About the author

Ann Wardlaw began her career as a teacher before switching to journalism. She has been a regular contributor to *She* magazine and has also written for national newspapers including the *Daily Mail* and *Daily Express*. Ann lived in France for many years, where she and her husband restored an 18th-century farmhouse, and she now lives in Wiltshire. Her first novel, *Diamond Pitt*, was published by Book Guild in 2014.

By the same author

Diamond Pitt, Book Guild Publishing, 2014

SHADOWS OF YESTERDAY

Ann Wardlaw

Book Guild Publishing

First published in Great Britain in 2015 by
The Book Guild Ltd
9 Priory Business Park
Wistow Road
Kibworth
Leics LE8 0RX
Tel 0800 999 2982
Email info@bookguild.co.uk

Typesetting in Sabon by
Keyboard Services, Luton, Bedfordshire

Printed in Great Britain by
CPI Group (UK) Ltd, Croydon, CR0 4YY

A catalogue record for this book is available from
The British Library.

ISBN 978 1 910508 24 4

And all our yesterdays
have lighted fools
the way to dusty death

William Shakespeare, *Macbeth*

Dedicated to 'Georges' and his group of Bretonne Résistants, whose courage and endless bravery helped in ending the enemy occupation of France, freeing thousands from unbelievable terror until liberty was achieved.

1

1966

Marc Chevaud eased his long, slim body against the seat of the dining-room chair until he felt more comfortable. The chairs were hard and horribly practical, unlike most of the furniture to be found in his sister's large house in leafy Surrey. Only recently had his sister and her family moved there from a smaller house near Winchester.

Gazing round at the now familiar surroundings he could not help smiling a little. How well he knew Simone! It was all Simone, he concluded, as he thoughtfully studied the oval miniature of himself on the wall above the fireplace. He was staring at the past, his own faded figure, dressed in the uniform of a Lieutenant of de Gaulle's Free French Army, which looked back at him with a sombre, fixed expression. At that very moment, he felt as if he was looking at a vague spirit of the past.

Why could he not forget past events? Perhaps because they really were heinous, despicable works belonging to an army of sadists. Acts of unforgiveable behaviour towards harmless, innocent people, including small children and the frail elderly. The innocents were inhabitants of remote hamlets, where yesterday was an interminable, long day and for many there would be no tomorrow.

In spite of himself, Marc could not forget, and once again the events of a particular day overtook his mind.

A heavy column of armoured transport moved in mechanical

1

deliberation, causing damage to the mountain road and snaking its way past stone wayside huts, covered with a sprinkling of snow. In peacetime, occupants often sold cool, welcome drinks to tourists and hikers alike. Holes in the road were causing havoc to the occupants of half-track vehicles, men in Tiger tanks laughed at stricken comrades who were thrown about as they attempted to make shells safe for use during the impending operation.

Leaving Cahors behind, Marc dragged himself back to the present, hating what he was remembering, loathing his own photographic image – it was all disgusting. Then, he had been without knowledge of what was leading up to the worst massacre of civilians in World War II, fuelling the flames of anger that still burned with tremendous force through most of France. Memories were long and deep.

Yes, he too was a part of Simone and not just the elder brother who had acted as a guardian and protector since her adolescent years. Now she was the one who was doing the caring. She pampered him, watched him, cared for him and, in many ways, she fussed him, which he, at last, grudgingly, accepted.

He looked away from his dark outline and listened to the noises from outside. He was alone from choice, they had all deserted him, with the exception of an over-indulged Siamese cat, which lay preening itself in the early afternoon sunshine. The family had gone to finish a game of croquet, begun long before lunch. It seemed that he and the cat shared a mutual disinterest in any form of exercise at that moment. The cat dozed and Marc slipped into an interlude of dreams, disturbed by the sound of mallet striking ball, and the intermittent crack of a gun being fired in the field below the garden. It had no effect on the multitude of rooks as they swarmed about the recently harvested field.

Charles had insisted that the game of croquet be finished, and armed with a well-worn mallet had marched outside to the lower lawn, the rest meekly following. Marc likened his brother-in-law to a cavalry officer taking to the polo field. Charles! Backbone of England, but by no means spineless, married to a chic, vivacious creature and creating something almost beyond the realms of perfection.

He could hear them outside, Simone's gentle laugh, trailing off into a school-girlish giggle, coupled with the grunts of an ever-mindful husband, who treated her with the same careful dominance he exerted over his children when mild parental discipline was needed. Reaching out, Marc lifted a glass slowly from a side table, held it to his nose and slowly inhaled the bouquet with an air of expert judgement. Suddenly, quite contrary to the expertise he appeared to possess, he tilted back his head and tossed the Armagnac down his throat in one decisive gulp. His movement was a defiant gesture against another noise he heard outside; he had become used to the rook-scaring machine and the sound of wood on coloured balls, the occasional giggles of Simone and the deep rumbling chuckling of Charles. This was the seductive, unnerving laugh of his sister-in-law Karin, his brother Leo's attractive wife, who was aware of her incredible beauty. Leo did not see anything other than her beauty; she was just a woman, and a useful excuse helping to disguise his preferences for those of his own sex.

A box of best Havana cigars had been left for Marc by his side. Reaching out, he selected one. Move number two – the second defensive action in his war. How to overcome his problems of guilt regarding Karin. Why was it, he thought, as he fingered the smoothness of the leaf, that she disturbed him to the point of frustrated exasperation? Why indeed, he mused, as he struck a match and waved it across the end of the cigar several times.

The blueness of the smoke, the mildness of its aroma, captured his thoughts as they pervaded the room, and briefly his mind left family patterns and interruptions. Perhaps it

3

was autosuggestion, the cigar, the sunshine, the softness of the pale brown tobacco, firm beneath his fingers, that reminded him of his seduction by a woman, the initiation of the seventeen-year-old virgin he had been at the time. It was France, the warmth of the Mediterranean, and all the things associated with home.

Home! With resignation, he had accepted a long time ago that he was homeless; doesn't the expression say 'home is where the heart is'? His heart was in France. Dear, beautiful France; childhood memories flooded his mind, his beloved mother, the village, everything about the chateau where he had been born, which was now falling into ruins after being occupied by Nazi troops. His nostalgia was destroyed. Karin laughed again and the dog barked – perhaps it had bitten her? After all, the animal had suffered with the rest of them, having endured a lunch lasting over two hours. It had also tolerated the trite conversation they had all managed to pour from their full mouths, with the help of generous servings of wine.

A less worldly gentleman might have assumed that Karin was typical of her class. Even Leo, after eight years of marriage, seemed to be blind to her faults, or if he did notice them, cleverly brushed them aside as part of her original charm. There was certainly something original about her. Leo had once remarked, when a little drunk, that she possessed a 'unique touch'. Marc, too polite to press his brother for an explanation, had remained silent.

He left the chair and stood by the open window. There was no movement of air. The beech trees stood like pale granite posts, their leaves yearning for the vapours of heaven. More relaxed, he returned to his armchair, and within seconds was asleep.

The sound of disturbed rooks from the plantation of oaks cut into his subconscious, bringing back grotesque and terrible memories of 1942, when the Germans had occupied his home and his village, destroying everything they could and much of his pleasant life. It was as if he had become hypnotised. He was asleep and perfectly relaxed, yet at the same time was aware of what was around him. In the heat of the afternoon everything was still, nothing moved. The dog lay panting in the shade of a rosemary bush, its tongue the colour of Simone's young hothouse carnations.

During his journey into the past, sleep had overcome him, and Simone crept into the room to draw the curtains. The scent of potpourri was pleasantly noticeable. In a far corner, she looked at him stretched in an armchair, his long legs out in front of him. Deciding he should rest, she left him in what she assumed was peaceful abandonment.

How wrong she was! His trance-like condition forced a small vision, which developed into a picture of immense panoramic beauty, becoming alive. The silver slopes fell away to find their own level in a shallow bowl of the valley. The moonlight seemed to sparkle. The farmhouse, on one side, with its crooked chimney and tumbled roof, gazed up with respectful civility at the solidness of the chateau. Their positions created in an abstract manner, a class distinction between stone, mortar, glass and paint.

Was that how it was? The peasants below struggling to exist while the more fortunate, living on a higher plain, looked down upon the servants of the soil. They watched, they ruled and they possessed, until the invaders arrived to change it all.

He remembered the nights when terrible things had happened. Try as he could, he was not able to blot out the ghastly images in his mind. They had received orders to occupy the plateau, but the message had not been clear. The organisation had miscalculated the number of enemy soldiers. Marc's group was far too small to be a worry to the enemy – they were insignificant.

He, Philippe, Remy and a few others lay hidden from view behind a large collection of rocks, watching the enemy and counting the troops as best they could, with the help of powerful binoculars. Dawn brought an eerie silence after a night of noise from German vehicles and infantry. Snowflakes began drifting in the mist which crept across the plateau and Marc felt the dampness on his already cold hands and face; it was bitter. Fingers on the trigger of his gun had become numb, with pins and needles attacking his feet with a vengeance. The half-tracks trundled on.

'They're on the move,' Philippe said, longing to light a cigarette, but he dared not risk it.

'OK,' Marc replied in a hushed voice.

Silent, menacing shrouds of mountain mist encroached towards the plateau, a heavy stillness, destroyed by weary battle-scarred troops. The day before, 5,000 German troops had arrived, with a huge assortment of artillery. After the first frenzied attack, the Maquisards lost over 100 men. But German losses were also high. Two hundred bodies lay, barely visible, buried in cold, clinging clouds of vapour. Like blessing the bloodied earth, as a priest swung a censer, sanctifying the souls of the dead. For the shivering, huddled Resistance, the mist was a gift, helping to hide them, before finalising their next attack.

It was different for the enemy. The murkiness hindered them in their quest for revenge after the killing of over 200 of their comrades in a previous skirmish. Flares lit up the plateau, as shooting stars blazed away to a celestial venue, cutting through the showers of grey fog with a brilliance of vibrant colour.

It was time! Marc nudged Philippe to pass on the message. They knew what had to be done and the huge strength of their adversaries. Only 200 metres separated the Mayor's house from the Salon de Féte, which had been commandeered by the SS (*Schutzstaffel*) and used as a prison camp, its occupants consisting of women and children. Between the noise of German artillery, cries from terrified victims could still be heard. Marc's group had to free them after killing the twenty-odd guards. Typical! he concluded, so many armed men to oversee women and children, to beat them with rifle butts, starve and rape them.

No one had told him of the barrier of dense razor-wire, but it was too late. He signalled his group to halt and turn back. Philippe stumbled, catching his left foot in a discarded tyre, trapping himself as he fell forward, head first into a wall of wire. The rusting spikes cut into his face, tearing at flesh. He closed his eyes for protection and lay still in the cold darkness of the night.

Marc knew it would be a formidable task to rescue his friend. Without any form of light he too was caught, trapped. He reprimanded himself of his own foolish decision not to use gloves. Numbed fingers were impeding his use of wire cutters. Pressing triggers was also not easy. It took three men to release Philippe and drag him away, reaching the safety of the rocks, as Nazi guns began to fire. High above them, a Luftwaffe bomber decided to release bombs on the plateau. Flames shot into the air, enabling Marc to see the silhouette of the school building and the soldiers leaving, and he cursed.

The Germans, sensing that their advance was made easier with the bombers' help, quickly advanced towards the village, rounding up everyone they could find. They herded prisoners to waiting lorries, ignoring the females, leaving them in the school to burn to death.

With unbelievable strength and ingenuity, Marc returned to the gaping hole in the barbed wire. He and his followers ran to the back of the school, releasing as many women and children as possible. All were in deep shock and had to be conveyed outside towards the church, which thankfully was still undamaged. Marc shuddered as one elderly woman and another, holding a baby in her arms, ran into the building and hid behind the altar, while the mother stifled the child's cries with shaking hands, as Marc's eyes were blinded by a mixture of smoke and tears.

Triumphant shouts from the Germans could be heard. The old lady opened a side door leading to a desecrated graveyard, where decapitated angels with their broken wings lay in the now drifting snow. Calling to the mother, she shouted for her to throw out the small baby from the window above. It was some time before Marc heard the child had died from its injuries. Ironically, its mother survived.

When the end came, many were past caring and a strange complacency overtook them. Lawless citizens, in a state of shock, had fallen out of love with their own country and life itself. They had fought as nationals, and now nationalism was more dead than alive.

2

Marc's face creased in a half-smile. He had the best of both worlds. What he was thinking was not imagination. It existed. It was all fact, true, but frightening. It was all true except for one thing, one facet he had allowed himself to add; the missing piece of the puzzle, a piece as elusive as the spider his youngest nephew, at that moment, was attempting to imprison in a matchbox. Piers, aged eight, was losing the battle, eventually throwing the empty box into a border of summer flowers.

Sylvie! Always when given the opportunity to indulge in the dreams of home, he permitted Sylvie to travel with him. There was never anything immoral about their journeys. Somehow, try as he might, he could never become totally involved with a young girl he now knew only in his imagination. But she was there! His first love; a child of innocence and full of youthful charm. She was not like Simone. Yet there was something about her that he often felt related more to Karin. Yet Sylvie was unsophisticated, unpolished, unused.

How could she be like Simone, even as a child? He hardly knew Simone's childhood days for he was trying to fight a war, with a band of exiles in what seemed to be a foreign country, now alien to him, while his sister lay safely cocooned in the cotton-wool world of a convent. A world of cold, grey stones and black cloth, the texture of the two materials as cold and remote as the bells that the Sisters of the Cross rang each day on the appointed hour. Strange that Simone had not become indoctrinated by the insularity of life behind the convent walls.

Sylvie was the one luxury he allowed himself to take when he returned to the place of his birth. Fantasy, he knew, was a means of escape, and no right was needed to indulge, but for him, the dreams he owned, the dreams he clung to, had become an obsession. He had one continuous nightmare. As sleep came swiftly, he surrendered easily, enjoying total relaxation, yet his vision continued to its full extent, taking him on a terrifying journey. Once more, he rode the big black night horse, his anger and fear, a mixture of terror and hatred.

The young became obsessed with ideas. He was not young by any means but until recently would have pushed away the thought of being old as foolish. He had to decide whether he was becoming over-sentimental, even blind, to the day-to-day management of the industrial empire he now controlled. Was he, at the age of forty-five, allowing sentiment, even senility, to set in, to take the place of the hard efficiency expected and required always from the Managing Director?

It was destroying him. It had always been there, but now it was like a blemish one suddenly noticed on the skin. It could be covered, camouflaged or surgically removed, but it usually returned, and when it came back it irritated and grew, until it could no longer be ignored. If only he could talk to someone about it. There were thousands like himself who had suffered brutality, imprisonment, torture; they would understand. Philippe Coutanche, the bailiff at the chateau, knew and empathised, having been a victim of Nazi callousness. Those in other prisons were not so lucky, all were executed.

The Allied invasion was coming – they knew this, as did the enemy, however, the plateau's many narrow paths were still blocked by snow. German forces, aided by several thousand hated Milice, assembled at the foot of the plateau. Three hundred Resistance managed to escape from the fighting. However, many died, some, after being hunted down, were killed in reprisals of barbaric consequences. The Maquisards felt hope as they hung on for the much-awaited D-Day invasion. Their morale was great despite a lack of ammunition and supplies.

Marc did not see the German Corporal who pushed a gun into his back. He knew it was madness to run or put up a fight. He was imprisoned in Paris, sent to Mont Valérien prison, awaiting execution with other compatriots. There he was given news of the hostages taken at Oradour-sur-Glane; seventy-nine innocent men had been hanged in public from lampposts, they were not Resistance or Maquisard, and the guard who gave him this information was laughing as he broke the news. Suddenly, after a few days, the killing ceased. The guard did not tell him this, the joke was on the French. Word went round that the assassins had run out of rope – not enough left over to hang themselves. Marc thought a further batch of 300 Resistance had been taken to Limoges, some of them to certain death in the Dachau concentration camp, leaving no evidence.

Enraged by the humiliation of the successful attempts made by the Maquisards, the Germans were filled with a desire for revenge for their own losses. They occupied many innocent villages and, once again, Marc's guard laughingly informed him that the number was about 3,000 killed. Oradour was set on fire, no one was left alive – the 600 inhabitants were murdered, including 200 children. Marc's rage was under-standable, but he was helpless to assuage it, or take revenge.

The Americans, British and some Russians were there and he waited in Mont Valérien for almost certain death, with hundreds of others. Realising the end was near, the Gestapo were shooting all prisoners. The atmosphere had completely changed. Guards and soldiers no longer marched down the cold concrete corridors, their boots clattering, accompanied by urgent shouting. Marc wet his index finger from the bottom of a tin mug containing a little water, and traced a cross on the cell door. With difficulty, he knelt on the cold uninviting floor and prayed for strength and guidance. In all his time as a 'terrorist' (to state the title given him by the SS), he had never thought of dying. Was this his appointed date with death? A beating of boots, his door was viciously kicked open and two stone-faced guards glared at him, breathing heavily.

'*Raus, Raus! Schwein, Schwein!* '

Marc, still on his knees holding on to the door jamb, pulled himself up cautiously and edged his way between the guards, expecting a punch in the face or an assault. He sidled into the corridor and stood there, uncertain what to do. Nothing happened! He shuffled to the exit and waited for the door to be unlocked. Astonishingly, it was pulled open from the outside. His amazed face was met by a British Army Captain, who ordered others behind him to enter the building.

'Come on! Let's get the rest,' he said. Turning to Marc, he asked, 'What shall I do with these bastards?'

'Shoot them,' Marc said. 'Or I will if you give me a weapon.'

The Captain smiled sardonically. 'Come, come sir, that isn't allowed. The Geneva Convention and all that.'

'Everything is allowed in here,' Marc replied. 'Everything that is wrong, wicked, or cruel. My colleague, Philippe Coutanche, is he alive?'

The Captain shook his head. 'Can't say, there's bodies all over the place outside the wall. Follow me,' he said, 'I think I know the way.'

'So do I,' Marc said, 'blindfold.'

The corpses lay in piles as if they were in a cold embrace. Philippe was alive, chained to a wall that had been sprayed with machine gun bullets.

'We've no wire cutters,' the Captain said.

'Just give me your revolver,' Marc responded, holding Philippe's hand and pressing it to his face. 'He's still alive!' Marc spoke with relief.

'Am I dead?' Philippe's voice, a broken whisper.

'Yes and I am the Devil,' Marc replied. 'You lucky old man. Who will tend my vines if you're not around?'

Philippe's eyelids fluttered. 'Take me home,' he murmured, 'and make sure you have some cognac ready. I am so very tired.'

Years later, when giving evidence as a witness at a Nuremburg hearing, Marc learned the truth about Oradour, those he had tried to save with help from friends and members of his patriotic group. He still lived with the horrors and the trauma many others had experienced. How he wished he could develop a state of amnesia. Unfortunately, he still had many associations; his dear friend Philippe and his own village of Mirabeau, still beautiful, except for the family's ancestral home, Chateau Nuage. Now numerous ghosts walked in the former elegant rooms, sending faint whispers of cold air down the beautiful staircase, which had once been a perfect example of magnificent rococo design.

Marc and Philippe had agreed to spend a little time in Paris on their return journey home, and there was official transport laid on for them. It had been Philippe's suggestion, not wholly accepted by Marc, but whose wish was to make Philippe happy.

Over an aperitif in a bar they discussed the day's events, joked about the enemy now on trial, pleading for their lives, lying through their teeth, and saw how they were visibly shaking. They shared an identical conclusion. It was then Marc told Philippe of his intentions, to return to the UK and manage the problems that his company, Cheval Zips, was experiencing.

'But when will you return to us here? You have seen the damage, there are problems at Mirabeau too!'

'Yes, but if I don't sort out Cheval Zips, I cannot help Mirabeau and my rightful home.'

After minutes of silence and playing with his empty glass, Philippe said, 'They'll have to pay you compensation and that will take years.'

'Maybe,' was the reply. Marc was watching a young woman standing at the zinc, drinking some wine. From the back, her hairstyle reminded him of Karin.

Karin! Another time, another place, another world. Her world was collapsing and falling into pieces, like his, but his he hoped to save. He could not rescue Karin from the misery Leo had caused, and in which she was expected to live. It did not matter as much as it may have done in the past.

Respecting one's elders and their behaviour throughout the war – for a long time talk in the bars and in the fields would be of their own horror stories of the long conflict. Sometimes, many of them would prefer not to talk at all.

Was it his dream that made him empty inside? Marc had everything, yet nothing. As head of the family, he had power, and as head of the family business, he had superiority. He was the Comte de Mirabeau, king of an enigmatic empire, manufacturing the world's best-selling zip fasteners. It was enigmatic because no other company seemed able to produce anything equally acceptable or effective. Cheval Zips – or as a friend once remarked, 'horse flies with the sharpest sting'.

The vision of Sylvie, basking in complete innocence, made him feel good. Sometimes he felt as if he were a completely fulfilled man. Sometimes. That was a rare occurrence.

How could he do it? What reason could he give to Simone and Leo? How could he explain that he wanted to go away? Simone would say she understood, but she was always ready to tolerate his whims and fancies without questioning his motives. Besides, he was almost old enough to be her father. He hoped she understood, fundamentally, what his innermost desires were, even if he never mentioned them.

She had always been so understanding. He could not remember one instance when she had tried to tell him what to do. Not once had she ever questioned his movements, but why should she? He was sixteen years her senior. He was Marcus, her older brother, and he was special. He might not be God, but to her, he was certainly divine.

And Leo? The man who never quite made it, but was still trying; the apathetic younger son with a chip of solid lead on his narrow shoulders. Insecure, although aware of his responsibilities, always fighting the odds, which to him seemed overwhelming, the highest being a young wife, whose merits appeared to rest solely on her ability to let men make fools of themselves.

What if he went to Leo, now, that very minute, and said that he was going away? Leo's reactions would be as clearly defined as the shape of the chair in which Marc sat. He would welcome the suggestion, forgetting for a while the idea he had that Marc permanently overshadowed him. Leo persecuted himself with a fixation that Marc's superiority in both age and practical knowledge stopped him from being a real person.

Leo, although seven years younger and the middle sibling, was quite unpredictable on occasions, but here was a time when Marc knew exactly how Leo would react. Marc opened his eyes briefly. Nothing of importance had ever been delegated to Leo. He had escaped the agonies of war. Situations could be changed and Marc realised that he at last had come to a decision. Guilty of procrastination, now he was going home!

The cigar had long gone out. On his lapel, ash lay in a soft grey ringlet. About to stand and brush it into the empty hearth, he heard the voice of Piers, Simone's youngest son, calling him from the hall. Quickly he closed his eyes again. The child called several times, each time with a ring of new urgency in the tone.

'Uncle Marc!'

Marc remained motionless. He heard the footsteps, harsh on the wooden floor of the hall, becoming softer as they approached the carpet. He felt the boy's presence; heard the rapid breathing and almost felt the warmth of the thin arm, although it still had yet to touch him. Without opening his eyes, he knew exactly what kind of expression the young face conveyed.

'Uncle Marc!'

The small hand, its fingers digging into the material of his jacket, felt urgent. Marc could smell the slightly pungent odour of linseed oil. Perhaps the croquet had died a natural death and a test match been played, lost or even abandoned.

'Uncle Marc! We're all going to Wynn Hill. Papa wants to show Uncle Leo the new glider. Will you come?' As an afterthought, he added, 'Please.'

Marc opened his eyes and found himself looking into the freckled face of his nephew. The face was as open and free as the petals of the roses on Simone's desk.

'All right.' He stood, carefully brushing the lapel. 'When are you leaving?'

'Now,' Piers replied, running from the room, his sandals unbuckled, and the heels trodden down.

From where he stood, he could hear Simone's scolding tones.

'I distinctly told you not to disturb Uncle Marc and you deliberately disobeyed me.'

'But he wants to come,' the child insisted.

'No, he does not. You want him to come but he is very tired.'

'He's always tired,' Piers moaned.

There was a pause. Marc wondered what they were doing.

'Maman?'

'Yes?'

'Why do old people always fall asleep in chairs?'

'Go and wash your hands,' Simone ordered. 'And do up your sandals.'

Marc had not only heard the footsteps as they died away, but the words Piers had so truthfully used.

16

Was he old? He had to ask himself that same question so many times lately. There were moments when he felt that the passing years were having a pronounced effect on him physically.

He waited for Simone to enter the room. As she did so, he watched a smile break on her face. It never failed to move him, almost as if she knew how it boosted his sagging morale and helped in making him feel secure.

He had not realised until she bent down to kiss his forehead that he must have sat down again after Piers had left him.

'Piers thinks that anyone over twenty-one is ancient,' she said soothingly, stroking his lapel where the ash had been. 'Do you really want to come, or is it his own little idea?'

Marc looked at her, admiring the simple beauty. He put his hand up to lightly rest on hers.

'Would you mind terribly if I didn't?'

'No. I'd be delighted, if not relieved, Mano.' She automatically fell into the practice of using her pet nickname for him whenever they were alone. 'As a matter of fact, I'd rather you stayed. Leo and Karin are having one of their marathon rows and I think it much better if you stayed here.'

'I shan't stay here.'

'Oh.' She sat on the arm of the chair. 'Not even for tea?'

'I have some paperwork to finish. I'll have tea at the flat.'

He released her hand and eased himself from the chair. It moved slightly from its unbalanced position. She walked towards her desk and played with an invitation card.

'Have you seen this?' she asked, her back towards him.

'Yes,' he said, moving closer.

'I told Charles I didn't want to go, but he said it was one of those duty things and that I must.'

Marc smiled. 'Then you must, *ma petite*, mustn't you?'

'Yes,' she sighed. 'I suppose I must. Believe it or not, I dislike weddings.'

'This one does happen to be the daughter of our General Manager.'

17

She looked up and turned slightly. 'Are you going?'

'No,' he replied, 'I'm not.'

She turned and looked at him, her expression one of complete puzzlement. 'But you said F...'

'Never mind what I said.' He reached out and took the invitation from her, replacing it in its original position.

'I've already replied,' he said, 'declining, but enclosing a generous cheque.'

'Why?' Simone seemed put out by his decision. 'Charles can't get away. I was counting on you to pick me up and bring me back. Really, Mano, it is a bit much, expecting me to go all the way to Chester Square on my own. You know how I hate driving in town.'

'Go with Leo and Karin.'

'You still haven't told me why you aren't going.'

'I'm going away,' he said, and left her to stand staring a little despondently at the fallen rose petals on her desk.

3

He left Simone's without saying goodbye. There was no one around except the cat, who had moved with the sun and lazed on a windowsill, feigning sleep. He placed a note of thanks on the kitchen table, adding a postscript that he would telephone later that evening.

The countryside quickly faded and he found himself thirty minutes later in the slow lane. The Peugeot purred, content to allow the rest of the weekend traffic to overtake at high speed. Marc knew he could join in the dash for home, but his mind was occupied with other things. Like the car, he was no stranger to that particular stretch of road for it had become yet another pattern in his life to spend most weekends in the country. Simone smothered him and Charles fussed. They were both too sensitive to be cast aside, even for the weekend, and the last thing he wanted to do was hurt them. On reflection, two days at their house was infinitely better than a weekend alone in his London flat.

Although the music from the radio was soft, it disturbed his thoughts. This time he did not wish to have his concentration upset. He wanted to go over every detail; to wallow in the satisfaction he felt within. He wanted to gloat on his decision. It had not been an easy one to make. It was the culmination of the dream he had clung to for a long, long time.

In the Square, a slowly descending sun seemed to swallow up the windswept fallen petals which were scattered around the green centrepiece of lawn. It was empty of people but various cars were parked against the tree-lined pavement. Pulling up opposite the flat, he switched off the engine and got out, remembering to place his resident's parking disc on the windscreen, before locking the door.

He crossed the narrow street, a small case in one hand, a briefcase and rolled umbrella in the other. As he reached the top step, a spot of rain touched his face. He glanced upwards to see a sky not only preparing for night, but now suddenly heavy with thundery rain. It was then that the feeling of apprehension overcame him. Travelling back, he had been so sure. Now he was uncertain.

The small drawing room with its ornate ceiling felt dismal and humid, while the Adam grate was bare and cold. He thought how welcoming a log fire would have been, remembering the large ones at Nuage before the war. His eyes quickly inspected the room. Nothing out of place. He poured himself a drink, selected several books from a shelf and took them to a small sofa, where he sat down by the side of the empty hearth.

He was trembling due to the intense and excited feeling of anticipation – of going back to France. He drank the whisky, placed the glass on the floor, and then opened one of the books. The dark clouds were still gathering, not allowing sufficient light to read by; however, he had no intention of reading. The stiff cover presented a large and detailed map of France. With a finger he traced the Rhone and then the Durance. His eyes were beginning to close. He would have to tell Charles that late nights no longer agreed with him.

Perhaps Sylvie might come? He was drifting. If she came, there would be renewed hope. And if there was hope, there would be courage.

She did not appear. He was completely alone.

He must have fallen asleep very quickly. A loud ringing brought him back to reality. Steadying himself against the mantelpiece, he tried to collect his senses. The bell went on ringing, as if the caller had jammed a finger in the button. He moved, kicking the empty glass with a numbed foot.

'All right,' he muttered, 'I'm coming.'

Karin stood swaying on the step, her arm against the bell. She looked at him with vacant eyes, through strands of black hair soaked from a sudden downpour. For one moment, he visualised her collapsing at his feet, and hesitatingly he put out a hand to catch her. The longing to take her in his arms was just bearable.

'You are going to ask me in, aren't you?' she said, her words slurred.

'Yes,' he said, opening the door fully. 'Of course.'

She staggered past him, her long cotton skirt swishing against the wall. He followed her, dimly aware of her clumsy movements in the darkened passage. She was drunk. He had seen her like this before at parties and business functions, where she usually embarrassed Leo and angered Simone, but this was the first time she had come to the flat on her own and in this condition.

He looked at his watch, pulled the curtains and felt for a lamp. It was not bright enough and he turned on all the lights, showering her with a brilliance she did not want. His action was a form of protectiveness against being alone with her in the dark.

'Please,' she said. 'Do you have to be so unkind?'

'I'm sorry,' he replied, and switched them off, leaving the lamp to smile in solitude at the shadows it was casting on the wall. 'Would you like something for your head?'

'I haven't got a head but you could offer me a drink. I've always been led to believe that your hospitality is the finest in town.'

Ignoring the remark, he picked up his fallen tumbler and refilled it. For her, he took a smaller one and poured a measure of brandy.

'Here! Drink it slowly!'

She took the glass from his hand, peered into it and laughed. 'You can't be serious! There isn't enough to cover the bottom!' She tutted. 'You're worse than Leo.'

21

He stared at her, his expression hard. 'I think you've had enough.'

He studied her, aware that she could not see him clearly. In all the time he had known her, he had never been in this situation before. It was something he had always dreaded and carefully avoided. He and the rest of the family were aware of her weaknesses but had, from the beginning, remained hopeful that they could eventually mould her to their mode of life. His attitude was intentionally aloof. He mistrusted himself and she knew it. Karin was more than attractive and he, as a man, vulnerable. But she was his brother's wife and he believed he was a man of principle.

'Why didn't you go straight home from Simone's?' he heard himself ask, his voice less soft than usual.

'I did.' She had finished her brandy and held out the glass. 'Could I possibly have another?'

Reluctantly he gave her a second drink.

'Then why have you come here?' He sat on the sofa. She watched him, noticing how he crossed his legs and how his black Gucci shoes shone against the luxurious carpet.

'I wish you'd be a little less conservative,' she remarked.

'You haven't answered my question,' he said, conscious of her unsteady hand holding the glass. He saw how she had splashed some brandy on her red shirt and how she was ignorant of her clumsiness. The dark patch stopped spreading across her left breast.

'Because there was nowhere else to go.'

'I am surprised,' he said, lighting a cigar. 'I thought you had so many friends.'

'Friends!' She laughed a little, but it was not her normal laugh. 'Tell me Marc, what are friends? Who are friends?'

'I wouldn't know,' he replied, thinking of enemies. 'I have few but that's a status many businessmen share. We just make hostile rivals. How did you get here?'

Surprised, she looked at him sharply.

'In the car, of course.'

He dropped the cigar in an ashtray and jerked to his feet, before she had finished speaking. Going to the window, he pulled back a curtain and peered anxiously into the street.

'That was a little foolish. Anything could have happened.'

'Don't tell me you're concerned for my welfare.' She grinned, her smile vaguely impish. 'Are you, Mano?'

He shot round angrily. 'Don't ever call me that!' He spat the words at her.

'Oh, sorry! Now I have upset you. I must remember that there are special little loving phrases allowed only by certain people.' She paused. 'Your sister makes me sick. Did you know that? She thinks she's so perfect.'

'Be quiet,' he said. 'Leave Simone alone.'

'Don't worry. I will.'

He swallowed hard and looking at his hand saw how white it was and how it grasped at the curtain. Again, he looked into the street. There was no sign of either her car or Leo's.

'Where did you leave the car?'

'I don't know.'

'Don't be ridiculous. You're not that drunk.'

'I crashed it.'

'You did *what*?' He took two steps towards her, then stopped.

'Smashed it.'

A sigh of desperation escaped his lips. 'Where?'

She shrugged her narrow shoulders impatiently. 'Round the corner, somewhere.'

'Was anyone else involved?' he asked.

'Only a pillar box.'

He lifted the telephone. For a second he held the receiver loosely in his hand.

'What are you going to do?' she asked. 'Call the police?'

'I'm going to ask Leo to come and take you home,' he answered, dialling the first digit.

23

She vacantly wandered about the room, still a little lost. The flat was strange, the contents so obviously Marc's. There was a collection of fine books and several good oil paintings; the largest one was a portrait of Simone with her two sons, Piers and Crispin, when they were quite small, with his sister smiling, looking pretty.

She knew he was watching her and sorry she could not see his face. Men like Marc were not difficult to understand once the first barrier had fallen. The only difficulty was discovering how to remove the barrier.

Marc let the number ring, watching her; the slim figure quite still, as it waited. No imagination was needed to tell him what it was waiting for. He wondered how many other men had done the same. How long could he continue to hover?

Leo did not reply. Marc let it ring three more times before replacing the receiver. Suddenly she turned, fell onto the sofa he had so hurriedly vacated, and threw her head back on a cushion.

'I'm high! I'm all lit up! Have you ever seen a girl lit up before? Not like this, I bet you haven't.'

He picked up his glass and drank. He needed time to collect himself again. Where the hell was Leo? They must have had another slanging match and he had probably gone off in a state of despondency. It had happened before. It would go on recurring until either they compromised or she completely grew up. Grew up! He was deep in thought.

'Once I saw a girl "lit up", as you put it,' he said, his words barely audible.

'What was it? Gin?'

'No. It was schnapps. They forced her to drink it and each took turns to rape her, then poured more of it over her clothes and set light to them.'

'I don't want to hear things like that. I was too young to know when you fought your rotten war you keep talking about.'

'I never talk about it,' he said, his voice almost a whisper.

'You just never talk.'

'Then I must change the situation,' he said. 'Let me tell you about her.' He towered over her, his anger barely controlled. 'They let her scream and scream and a thousand feet below, helpless in the valley, a Resistance group crouched hidden in a cowshed, with their hands over their ears. There's a shrine there now, but stones and words won't ever bring her back, no matter how deeply they are engraved.'

'You were in love with her,' Karin's voice was now soft, with a hint of sympathy.

'When the snow has gone, you can see it from the valley,' was his reply.

'I want to go home,' she said, sensing for the first time his mood.

'That's exactly where you are going.' He pulled her from the sofa as he spoke. Her hand was warm and a little clammy. She clung to him as he led her to the door.

'You hate me, don't you?' she said, releasing her hand.

'No,' he replied. I wish I did, he thought.

In the street, he released the passenger lock of the car. She fell in and lay slumped back in the seat. He realised she was incapable of closing her door and got out to do it for her. As they drove away, she thought how alike he and the car were. Both sophisticated in appearance, each moving in a straight line, both products of a hard and cold business world she would never understand.

He drove round the square twice before turning into the street. The accident must have happened in close proximity to the flat. Karin had been in no condition to walk very far.

He soon found her car, just a few yards from where he had turned. It was on the corner of a mews, the offside front wing badly damaged. A small group of people had gathered around the bright red sports car, but he could see no sign of the police.

He did not bother to stop until they came to Harding Street, the modern block of flats where Leo lived in emotional chaos with his insecure, alcoholic wife.

He took the corner a little wildly, his one aim to get her behind her own front door before reporting the accident. The private car park beneath the apartment block was fairly full and he allowed the car in front to reverse. While waiting, he searched for her bag. He could not remember seeing her with one. She must have left it in her car. He swore under his breath. This would mean finding the porter and asking for a passkey. The last thing he wanted was to draw attention to her present state.

With some difficulty, he got her out and steered her into the building. The porter was standing by the door of his office. He gave Marc a discerning look as he made his request. Without speaking, he disappeared and returned with a key.

'Mr Chevaud has gone out, sir,' he said, holding out a hand, extending his nicotine stained fingers.

Marc nodded. 'I know. Mrs Chevaud isn't feeling very well. I'll return this in a few minutes.'

The flat was on the first floor. He felt it pointless waiting for the lift which hovered between the sixth and seventh. It meant wasting time. The porter's eyes were still fixed on them as they walked away. Although Karin appeared to have recovered slightly, Marc took her arm a little forcefully.

The heavy scent of one of her perfumes floated towards him in the slight draught created on opening the door of Leo's flat. Inside, he could see without looking too hard that there was evidence an argument had occurred. The clothes she had worn at Simone's lay on the floor. The heat was stifling and, now that the rain had ceased, he flung the windows open to let in a cool breeze. When he had finished, he realised she was not with him. He crossed to the bedroom. She was lying on the bed, moaning.

'Get into bed,' he ordered.

'I want Leo,' she moaned again.

'You've never wanted Leo.'

'How wrong you are,' she said, adamantly, rolling over to face him, her words and their tone resembling a spoilt child. 'I've always wanted him. He doesn't want me.'

He went to the foot of the bed and took a corner of the quilt. With one flick, he lifted it and covered her, noticing that she was still wearing shoes. Then he left her quickly, before she had time to say any more.

Sitting down, he made a note of what he had to do on the pad by the telephone. He gave the words careful consideration before reaching out and dialling the police. Later, he rang Simone and explained what had really happened and what he was going to do. He did not linger in his conversation with her, but said enough to make her understand. She could be relied upon to contact their lawyer, just in case Leo could not be found.

It did not take him long to pick up the scattered belongings Karin had thrown on the floor. He gathered them into a bundle and pushed them on a shelf in the nearest cupboard. With one final glance at her and satisfying himself she was asleep, he left the flat, the passkey firmly in his hand.

Halfway down the stairs he met Leo coming up. Marc, standing two treads above, felt a pang of sympathy shoot through him. Leo was smaller in build but had always been the athlete of the family. There was nothing energetic or even virile about him now. He seemed like an old man, his shoulders bent, his head lowered, with eyes following the stairs he was finding difficult to mount.

For the first time, Marc noticed the small balding patch on top of Leo's head. Leo, who had owned such a fine head of hair, was beginning to show signs of age or worry, or both. Marc wondered which was worse; baldness, or the grey strands now so visible at his own temples.

Leo lifted his head and moved up one stair. His face was

sallow, his expression one of weary desperation. He could not hide the surprise he felt seeing Marc a few feet above him.

'Marc! What's happened?'

'I'll tell you at the top.' Marc turned and began to remount the stairs. 'I had to inform the police.'

Leo groaned. 'Oh, God!'

'I had no choice,' Marc said. 'You must have known she was drunk.'

They stood on the first floor, in a corner by the lift. Only one person passed them, taking no notice of their hushed whispers.

'I'd better ring Harvey,' Leo sighed. 'After what you've told me, we'll need a solicitor.'

'Simone's already done that.'

'Shall I see if she's all right before we go to the police?'

'No.' Marc realised that Leo was not aware of the urgency. 'We must get to the police station. We can talk on the way.'

'I don't feel very talkative.' Leo began walking slowly. 'There isn't much I want to say.'

Marc was ahead of him. 'At the moment, I don't want you to. But tomorrow, you and I are going to have a long discussion.'

Tomorrow! Marc's words went round in Leo's already confused brain. He dreaded what the next day would bring. After all, it was only a continuation of the one he had just lived, and that, like many other days, was unhappily a time he wanted to forget.

Trying to sleep later that night, Marc attempted to fight off the feelings of defeat. A few hours before, he had made up his mind to go back to the home of his childhood. He had also perjured himself for the first time in his life.

How could he leave them? They were like children with

adult problems. He couldn't leave Leo to manage a business at a time like this. Leo had a crisis on his hands and was unable to cope alone. Marc had watched him at the police station, nervously licking his lips and chain-smoking. The arrival of Harvey had been timely.

Karin would probably be charged with one of the road traffic offences but there was no evidence to show she had been drinking in spite of the police suspicions being true. He hoped she would have her licence suspended for a time. Someone like Karin was always safer in a taxi. He smiled a little. Perhaps it was the driver who took the risk.

Her behaviour had always bothered Marc. Not for her own sake, but he worried for Leo. Where had his brother failed? Somewhere, Leo had fallen down. It was not difficult to see why Leo had married her. She was young and beautiful; wild with enthusiasm for life. Her flippant conduct pushed any thought of responsibility she should have owned onto the shoulders of others. She had married Leo for what he could give her. She thought he would give her everything. What was it then he had denied her?

Marc turned over and tried to see the problem in a new way. He approached it from his own direction, for he was involved. Why had he acted so dutifully? On the way to the police station, he had told Leo what to say and what not to say, while they waited for Harvey to give them advice.

He had not perjured himself for Karin or for his own ends. He had lied in order to make the aftermath less painful. His saving of the situation had been to protect Leo from any further embarrassment.

In the morning, he would go to Simone. He would let Leo work out half the problem and hope that Karin would agree to a few days in a nursing home where she could dry out and do a little thinking. He closed his eyes. Yes, Simone was the person to see. This whole thing needed another opinion from a woman's point of view. Simone would have had her outburst earlier on when she and Charles went to bed. Charles would have soothed her, offered advice in his usual positive way, and probably calmed her much later by physically taking her with a gentleness she found both satisfying and protectively comforting.

When he eventually dropped off into a light, tense sleep, Sylvie came to him. Her face smiled and she held out her tanned arms, which had long been blessed by the warmth of the sun. He awoke, the ache in his body profound. His wet limbs told him he had an erection. He expected to see her by the foot of the bed, bathed in the golden light of rapture.

All he saw was the grey light of dawn approaching.

4

Simone's house looked peaceful in the fresh light of the morning. A slight wind sucked at the golden leaves of the almond trees and the front lawn gazed at a pale blue sky, with an almost translucent stare after a night of steady rain.

Marc's arrival was expected but his timing unknown. He had left the flat very early, driving out of London in a less condensed amount of traffic than those moving in the opposite direction. The city was opening her empty streets to the masses again. Monday was the beginning of the invasion and London waited, hankering for the next evacuation.

He let himself into the hall, the door pushing against a school satchel and a pile of books.

Simone heard him. In her usual composed way, she went to greet him, kissing him on both cheeks. He could feel her earrings on his face and there was something nice about the way she wore her hair. She was still in a dressing gown. He had bought it in Paris a few years ago. He remembered he had sent Karin a similar one as well.

'Mano! Oh, I'm glad you're early! We've almost finished breakfast but I can soon get you some.'

'Thanks. I only want toast and coffee,' he said, following her down the hall.

'Charles is buried behind his daily sheets of pink,' she remarked, excusably. 'Piers is supposed to be cleaning his teeth. Darling...' She leant over Charles's shoulder. 'Marcus is here.'

Marc looked at the back of the newspaper. He could see that he and his brother-in-law were dressed in almost identical pinstripe suits. The only difference was that Charles wore no waistcoat, but an old school tie was much in evidence.

Charles looked up, his brown eyes deep and staring intently. 'Heard the news? Inflation!' he snarled, showing aggression from his profession as a Lloyds broker.

'I haven't had time,' Marc said.

'All these "pie in the sky" plans for prosperity. They're on about takeovers again. Bank rate will go down again, wait and see! Nobody's safe.'

Marc smiled. 'You'll be quite safe.'

Charles grunted. 'It's people like you they're after.'

'I doubt it.' Marc sat down and unfolded a napkin. 'We're too small.'

'Take a look at this index!' Charles went to pass him the paper.

'I'll glance through later.' Marc took a piece of cold toast. 'I've other things on my mind at the moment.'

'What? Oh, yes, of course.' Unperturbed, Charles went back to his page of figures.

Simone returned with fresh coffee. She hurriedly put it down and began to pour.

'Charles, all the reading in the world won't raise the dividends or save a falling market. You're both going to be very late.'

'Both?' He peered over the top of the paper. 'Marc's only just got here.'

'You promised you would take Piers to school for me. Last night! Remember?'

This time his eyes flickered. 'Last night! God, how can I forget last night!'

He pushed back his chair and, with the newspaper folded beneath an arm, went to where she was sitting. He kissed her, his quick embrace telling her, in a shy way, all she wanted to know. It was the same every morning for both of them. He, forcing himself to a brief demonstration of affection, in case he forgot he had an underwriting syndicate to run and became carried away by her softness and utter femininity; and she, knowing how he felt, trying to be the efficient wife, whose main concern was arranging her household tasks. Sometimes, it did not always work. He was grateful to Marc that morning.

'Where's Piers? Playing with something?'

'With a toothbrush, I hope,' she said, passing coffee to Marc.

Marc watched as Charles's hand moved along the back of Simone's chair. He saw how it fondled the shoulder, and he felt contented at the sight of the cautious intimacy he was witnessing. If only Karin and Leo had a relationship like that – then there would be no problems. No problems at all, but his envy was enormous.

'Bye darling.'

'Bye,' she replied. 'Home usual time?'

'A little earlier, I hope.' He kissed her again, on the top of her head, and then turned to Marc. 'I know you two want to talk. I'll see you later. Maybe we can have a drink before dinner?'

Marc nodded. 'Fine. Have a good day.'

Simone stood. 'I'll get your umbrella. I think you're going to need it.'

Marc could hear them, their voices low for the benefit of Piers who clattered down the stairs. Somehow, Marc thought, the child was making a protest, for the noise he made seemed more acute than usual.

Marc chewed thoughtfully and enjoyed the coffee. It was always unfailingly good.

Presently, she returned and joined him.

'No greeting from my nephew,' he said.

'He isn't very happy this morning,' she replied, taking the coffee pot in her left hand, devoid of rings.

'Are any of us?' he asked.

She sighed and refilled his cup, adding sugar. 'Bad night?'
'Yes. You too?'

She nodded. 'Even Piers. Charles and I had a tiff. It was more than a tiff. I think Piers heard us. What a way to start the week, even for an eight-year-old little boy.'

'So you had a row and threw your ring at Charles. Is that it?'

Her right hand immediately went to her left, feeling for the fingers. Why was he always so observant?

'I did *not* throw it. I *gave* it to him. Our tiffs are always conducted in a civilised manner.' She drank, watching and waiting for a reaction. It never came. 'Charles took a mental beating,' she went on. 'Oh, Mano! It makes me fume when I think how Karin behaves. All the disharmony and disruption. I tried so hard to make yesterday a nice day.'

'You tried a little too hard, *ma petite*,' he said. 'We must leave them alone.'

'That's what Charles said. He said we shouldn't interfere.'

'He's right.'

'But Leo is so *lost*, Mano.' She watched him over the rim of her cup.

He took a cigarette and lit it.

Someone walked across the kitchen floor and began banging pans on the draining board.

'That's Mary,' she said, resignedly. 'I'd better tell her I'll do the lunch. She has all the washing.'

He had not followed her reasoning. She could tell that by the way his brows knit together.

'It's Monday – wash day!'

'I should have brought my shirts,' he said. 'Next time, I'll remember.'

'Go into the lounge and play some music. There's another paper in there if you want to catch up on the news. You need to relax.'

She left him. He could hear her talking to the daily help.

After stubbing out the cigarette, he poured a final cup of coffee and retreated to the lounge, before anyone could accuse him of disrupting the regimented routine of cleaning and dusting.

Once again, he sat in the chair he had occupied less than twenty-four hours ago. It seemed much longer, he thought, playing with the teaspoon. Simone had suggested music. There was no music at that moment sweet enough, gentle enough, or deep enough.

Driving down, he had given all his attention to the things he wished to discuss with Simone. She appeared to think it only concerned Leo's domestic troubles. Marc knew that Charles was absolutely right. Leo and Karin should be left alone, but he knew that if he could help Leo in another way, the situation might possibly resolve itself.

As he waited, he felt less concerned. It was strange how she had mentioned their father on the telephone the night before. They had been discussing what had happened. She had muttered something about Leo being weak and then, to Marc's astonishment, had questioned whether Leo was like the father she could barely remember. The topic was one they never discussed. In the past, he had tried slipping in the odd remark because he felt she was too shy or too afraid to ask. Each time he brought it into the conversation, she would go off at a tangent, commenting on anything from the cost of new curtains to the children's next holiday.

He had lied to her on the telephone by saying that he did not know about paternal characteristics. He had been a young man when he and his father had last met. It was not a meeting anyway – it was a departure.

The memory was vivid, one he was unlikely ever to forget. His mother uncontrollably weeping, clutched Simone's arm, while Leo, a thin young boy of thirteen, held on to her for futile protection. He remembered the porters, the unshaven dockers who roughly handled their luggage, and a mass of people surging and shoving on the quay, fighting for the final spare places held back for foot passengers. Lastly, he could not forget the group of students who had travelled a great distance to see him off with loud cheers from sad faces. Those faces had no doubt grown old, like his own. Many of them had been executed in Mont Valérien prison along with hundreds of others, simply for being young and patriotic.

Simone had cried from the time they boarded the antiquated carcass of a fishing boat until it reached England. Leo had simply stared at the other passengers until Marc took him up on deck to be sick. They were surrounded by people, mostly of Jewish extraction. It was that which had first made him start to question his father's motives.

They were not Jewish. They were members of a so-called aristocracy; low down the ladder of distinction, their ancestors murdered during the Revolution, but nevertheless regarded as elite. Why then had they been packed off, suddenly and without much warning, to a foreign country, which, by all accounts, would be occupied itself in a short while? At the time, it did not make any sense. Even now, it was just plausible. The traitor William Joyce whined repeatedly on the radio as Lord Haw-Haw and his Nazi propaganda was a standing joke amongst the English.

Simone came back carrying a tray of clean glasses. He could hear the whine of the vacuum cleaner, fighting to be heard above the noise from a transistor radio. The situation was not new to him. He had it at the factory, his employees regarding non-stop music as part of their industrial rights. It did not matter that some of them couldn't hear anything beyond the drone of their machines.

'Drink, Mano?' she asked, taking the tray to a cupboard.

'Isn't it a bit early?' He glanced at his watch. It had stopped. 'I've only just finished my coffee.'

'What have you been doing? It's almost twelve!'

'Then I would ask you the same question. You must have had a very long bath.'

'No longer than normal. I've been in the kitchen preparing lunch. I was going to give you cold meat left from yesterday. I've changed my mind. Today you must be a peasant and content to have bread and cheese and fruit.'

'Good,' was all he could say.

She finished putting away the glasses. 'Now, what about that drink? The usual?'

'Please.'

He sat with his back to her. He heard the drink being poured and waited for the chink of ice. He knew when she was bringing it to him, as he could smell her perfume. Last night it had been Karin's. Hers was different, heavy, powerful, and evocative. Simone's was light and flowery. Suddenly he knew the secret of perfume. It had never dawned on him before that women and perfume were the same. One knew the personality by the perfume! It was not simply a question of femininity for him, but nostalgia of the gardens of Paris in full bloom and the grandeur and beauty of Nuage.

Simone sat opposite him on a low stool. He was surprised how young she looked with her hair loose, the tips touching her shoulders. When she lifted her glass and said *santé*, he noticed she was wearing her wedding ring again, plus a small gold signet ring he had given her on her twenty-first. It had belonged to their mother.

'Now,' she said, putting down her glass. 'We were talking about Leo.'

There was not much to say about Leo, Marc thought, offering her a cigarette. They grew apart during the war. The years of separation, those hit and miss, hit and run years, had turned them into two strangers. Leo had been young. He had been sent to a school where, Marc subsequently discovered, they had treated him as a refugee. Leo had arrived in England with only a small vocabulary, but in those war years, he learnt a lot and it wasn't only a new language.

'Marc, what's the matter?' She sounded concerned.

'I want to talk to you, but it isn't about last night. Oh, it concerns Leo, it concerns him very much, but it also involves us.'

She lit the cigarette and coughed a little. Normally she only smoked to be social. Now she felt the need of something in her hand. The childlike remark Piers had made the day before, about old people, had stayed in her mind. Marc was not old. He was in his mid-forties. That did not make him old. He was going grey, yes, but that made him look interesting and definitely suave. A lined face; evidence of his bitter war with all of its implications.

'Is it a big worry?' she asked, not daring to look at him.

'I don't think you could call it a worry, Simone. Duty, I believe is a better way of putting it.'

'You look serious and sound a little too earnest, as if you're going to tell me something dreadful.' She got up. 'I'm going to pour myself another martini. Want one?'

He shook his head and waited for her to get a second drink.

'I'm going home,' he continued, after she had sat down again.

'What do you mean?' Her eyes were full of bewilderment. 'You haven't been here for three hours or discussed anything, and now you say you're leaving.' She began to lift her glass, only to change her mind and put it down. 'Marc, are you well?'

'I said I was going, not leaving. For me, home is France. I'm returning to the Chateau Nuage.' He saw her face turn pale and quickly added, 'For a short holiday.'

She did not speak. Her bottom lip was trembling but she remained silent.

'Simone?' His voice held a pleading tone.

She made no reply.

He went to her and knelt before her. He had half expected this kind of reaction. It was one of the reasons he had made up his mind. In a vastly different way, she was as insecure as Karin and Leo.

'Simone, listen to me.'

'I thought this was your home, or one of them,' she whispered.

'No, *ma petite*. This is your home. It is the house you and Charles made into a home. It is where you have made roots, the two strongest being your sons. In other words, your family.'

'But you are part of my family, Mano. You are all I have.'

'That isn't true. You know it isn't.' He reached out his hand and took her glass. 'Here, drink this.'

She sniffed. 'I don't want it.'

'Then *I'll* drink it,' he said, sipping the much-needed cocktail. 'I'm only going for a few days. Think of it as a business trip.'

'I can't,' she said, 'because I know it isn't. It's all tied up with Leo. Aren't you going to tell me?'

'Of course I'm going to tell you. I can't go away if I don't.'

'Couldn't I come with you? We could take the boys. It would help Crisp with his French.' She glanced at him hopefully, but knew it was no use.

'I have to go alone. I need you here to keep an eye on Leo, to tell me how he's coping. There are ghosts I have to lay to rest.'

'You honestly believe that by going away, the situation will ease? Mano, if I didn't know you, I'd say you were running away from your responsibilities.'

The words stung a little. Was that what she really thought? He had never run from anything in his life, apart from bullets, the result now causing her to lean on him even more. He had always taken his duties seriously. First, the factory and the name, then her and Leo. She was not only his sister. She was a business partner holding fifteen per cent of the shares. At meetings, she was capable, with a flair for seeing ahead, her uncanny perception often saving them unnecessary expense. Away from that environment, she was an attractive woman, an excellent wife and mother.

Karin had miscalculated Simone's character when she had so scathingly remarked on her perfection. Simone lived up to the astrological points of her Geminian personality. She was slightly possessive, with a penetrating mind, the latter enabling her to discern hidden weaknesses in others. Her possessiveness was due to her own insecurity. If he left them all alone, perhaps they would benefit from his absence. It was a risk he had to take.

'I'm going *because* I am aware of my duties,' he said, his tone low. 'It will do Leo good to take over. Don't you see what I am trying to do? I have to give him a chance.'

'I see that, but why do you have to go to France?' She looked at him with an almost pleading expression. 'Why the chateau? Why not take a holiday elsewhere? A cruise would be nice.'

'Simone, I have to go.'

'Then tell me why. You never talk about the place. You've not been there, well, to my knowledge you haven't, since we all left France. You can't be interested in a crumbling mansion.'

'When mother and I last saw each other, I promised her I would go back. It is my inheritance. One day it will belong to Crispin. Leo won't have any sons.' He paused, 'Actually, I've been back to the village several times.'

'What about your own sons? You might get married.'

'Do you understand now?' he asked, pushing aside her statement.

'Only that if you promised mother, I suppose you must. You won't actually stay in the house, will you?'

'Yes.'

'Marc, the place is probably in ruins. You'd be better off staying at an hotel in the nearest town. You could stay at that lovely hotel in Arles near the Roman ruins.'

He tried to hold back the quiet laugh, but it came out as a slightly suppressed burst. She could be forgiven for her innocent remarks and suggestions. For her it was just another name, a place on a map of the land which would have been proud to call her a daughter, but of which she silently denied any real knowledge. Nuage was on the outskirts of Mirabeau, a village in Provence, a vast area betrayed by Pétain to become Vichy. To Simone, it was as remote as the Antarctic. Perhaps as cold.

It was only a small village with one bar, the bakery, a church and a school. A collection of huddled houses clinging to the sides of a small hill. The occasional tourist found his way there, usually by accident, and bought a day's fishing rights. Seated by the bank of the river, he nearly always fell asleep in the warm sunshine; his closed eyes obscuring any vision he might otherwise have had of the aspiring artist, who followed in the tracks that Van Gogh and other artists had taken, when not possessed by a bout of madness.

'Marc, please don't stay there. You've no idea what state it's in.' She suddenly touched his hand. '*Is* it in ruins?'

'I really don't know,' he answered. He squeezed her hand. 'That's one of the reasons I have to go. You don't understand, do you? It is a very complex situation.'

'I don't wish to,' she said flatly. 'It has nothing to do with me. Besides, you're the head of the family. You make the decisions.'

How right she was, he thought, gazing at her. Her fair hair had fallen across her face, covering the wide brow and denying him the view of her large, grey eyes.

'Is Leo coming here today?' he asked.

'He'll phone. If he doesn't, I'll meet you both in town tomorrow. I can get my hair done.'

She moved her legs, unwinding them slowly. Then she stood. 'I think I'll get lunch,' she said, walking away before he could answer.

5

Marc waited for Leo and Simone at the corner of a crowded bar. Arms were knocked, drinks spilled, and occasionally there was an apologetic grunt from a businessman, juggling with a plate of sandwiches.

Leo used the place regularly, his choice silently making Marc question the reason. It was very much a venue for men and he was not happy that Simone had arranged to meet them there for lunch. She would appear incongruous; surrounded by shirts with stiff white collars, the Victorian hat-stand groaning beneath the weight of wet macs and rolled umbrellas.

He saw Leo arrive through a mass of bodies mingling around the door. Another few inches and they would find themselves in the street. His height helped him to be conspicuous and no signal was required. Leo saw him, nodded, and pushed his way towards the corner.

'I'm a bit late, sorry,' he said, undoing the buttons on his mac.

'Give me your raincoat,' Marc suggested, 'I can reach the hanger from here.'

He took the damp mac, his long arm stretching out to place it on the one remaining unoccupied hook. Leo brushed back his hair and then pulled at his tie.

'Has Simone arrived?'

Marc could not hold back his surprise. 'You knew she was meeting us?'

'Yes. I rang her last night, just after you left.'

'She was expecting you for lunch yesterday.'

'That's why I rang. I had to see to Karin. Let me get you something to drink.'

They stood by the wet coats, their backs against the bar. Their conversation was puerile. Marc longed to sit and talk about business but knew it was out of the question until a table became available and Simone had joined them.

He noticed the lines beneath Leo's eyes and glanced over his brother's shoulders to a mirror fixed on the wall. His own face showed signs of strain, but Leo's was haggard. It was interesting to watch him. Leo was oblivious to the fact that he was being intently scrutinised.

'What's happening?' Marc said, turning his head slightly and no longer facing the reflection in the mirror.

'I took her to a nursing home yesterday. She's sedated. The doctor said she must have complete rest from everything. Then she has to do detox.'

So that's it, they're going to dry her out, Marc thought, but noted the emphasis Leo had stressed when speaking the final word.

'And the accident?'

'Harvey says they might have her for due care and attention. We'll just have to wait and see.' He looked down at the tankard he was holding with both hands. 'Marc, was she...' he paused. 'Was she very tight?'

'She wasn't paralytic, if that's what you mean. She'd just had enough.'

'But not enough to satisfy her.'

Inside Marc felt the pity once more. At the same time, he admired the loyalty Leo obviously held for his wife. Condemnation was, he thought, a terrible thing.

'How long, Leo?' His voice was low, almost hushed, and lost in the babble of surrounding conversation.

'What?' Leo lifted his tankard. 'Oh, the drink? Only a few months really.'

'Any idea why?'

Leo's eyes narrowed. 'Funny, the doctor asked me the same question. I'll give you the same answer. I drove her to it.'

The hum of conversation stopped. Automatically, Marc's eyes watched the door. Simone had entered, clutching some parcels and bags. He waved and she smiled. The hum began again; several pairs of hostile eyes followed her as she pushed her way towards them.

'Tomato juice,' she said without waiting to be asked.

'Aren't you going to greet us?' Marc said, conscious that they were being watched.

She kissed Leo first. Remaining in the same position, she touched his cheek once, then standing on her toes she waited for Marc to bend down, before brushing her lips against his face. As Marc straightened, he saw the head waiter beckoning them through to the restaurant.

'Our table is ready,' he said. 'You can have your juice as a starter instead.'

Amidst the authentic Victorian furniture and decor, they talked earnestly for what seemed like hours, Leo, Marc observed, losing his reserve gradually, as the food and wine took effect. When Marc put the key question to him, he patiently waited for a reply. Leo's face did not alter but there was softness, hitherto undetected, in his voice.

'You want to leave me in charge?' He lit a cigarette and reached for an ashtray. 'It's a hell of a responsibility.'

'You think I don't realise that? I've had it for too long to know any different. The thing is, I know you can do it and I want you to do it. I'm only going away for a few days.' He was sorry that he was lying to them. His planned visit to France could easily last a few months, perhaps longer.

'He hasn't had a proper holiday for years, Leo,' Simone interrupted sympathetically, coming to Marc's defence.

'When are you going?'

'Next week. I've written to Coutanche telling him.'

'Coutanche?' Leo frowned deeply. 'Isn't he the bailiff at Nuage?'

'Yes,' Marc said, reaching out his hand as the waiter brought the bill to the table. 'Didn't Simone tell you? I'm going back to look at the old place. Not exactly a holiday.'

'You're mad! Surely there are better places to go?'

'I tried to tell him,' Simone said, 'but he appears to have made up his mind and we both know what that means.'

Marc stood and reached for his wallet. He watched Leo help Simone from her chair, then slowly made his way to the cashier's box.

As Simone waited, he whispered, 'Your hair looks nice.'

She turned round. 'Do you think Charles will notice?'

Marc smiled. 'Yes, but he won't say so. You know Charles.'

Outside the restaurant, they stood beneath the striped blind, wishing the rain would stop. Marc had no intentions of going to the office that day. Leo had an excellent excuse but had not said very much. He anticipated an afternoon vigil at Karin's bedside.

'Well, rain or no rain, I must finish my shopping,' Simone said. 'Charles has invited his parents for dinner tonight and I'm only happy about the main course.'

Leo swung round. 'There's a marvellous delicatessen on the next corner. They sell excellent cheeses.'

She touched his arm. 'Leo! You're so clever! Come with me!'

They walked away, temporarily forgetting Marc. Suddenly, she remembered and ran back to join him on the pavement.

'Marc, come and help choose.'

He did not move. She reached him and smiled. 'Come on, Mano! I want to keep his mind off things. Anything to help him, poor little devil.'

'Keep him occupied while I see the travel agent and collect a few things en route.'

'You really are going through with it?'

'Yes,' he said softly, looking across the street.

She gazed into his eyes but knew that he was only half conscious of her presence. 'Yes,' she sighed. 'You really are. Well, that's that. Don't let Leo spend the evening alone.'

He was touched by her concern for Leo.

'Don't worry. He can stay the night with me. Shall I get you a taxi?'

'No. I'll tell him to go back to your flat when we've finished.' She stepped back. 'Ring me in the morning.'

He did not turn round. She touched his hand and then abruptly left him, her heels tapping on the pavement.

Marc was a little surprised to see Leo turn up at the flat. After leaving him, he had used the time shopping and arranging last-minute details of his trip, yet he found himself thinking about his brother.

Leo too had been deep in thought. Simone in her usual effectual way had chatted throughout the entire shopping spree, purposely avoiding the topic which had troubled him so much earlier in the day. In Bond Street, he had left her in a taxi, waving to her as she disappeared in the direction of Piccadilly. He stood on the kerb staring into the distance. Then he turned and headed for Marylebone, so pensive that he did not even realise it had stopped raining.

He did not want to return to his own flat. He knew Marc would understand. Throughout lunch, he had felt Marc's eyes on him, that penetrating look which either told everything or conveyed nothing. Today it had told him everything. He felt somehow, for the first time in several years, within reach of beginning to know his brother. Simone likened Marc to a god, but Leo suspected that a devil hovered in and around those imagined beliefs. His brother was a dark horse, sometimes too secretive.

Marc let him in and showed him into the kitchen. 'I thought

we could start off out here, as we can talk without being disturbed by the telephone.'

Leo threw his mac over a chair. 'You've had the floor re-done,' he said, glancing at the tiles around his feet.

'That shows how long it is since you were here. I'll make tea, or would you prefer something else?'

'Tea will be fine,' Leo answered, lighting a cigarette and lolling back in his chair. He watched Marc, observing the manner in which he worked as he made the tea. Everything was meticulously done. Was this a reason for Marc's seemingly obvious choice of remaining a bachelor? Leo wondered if it *were* from choice. His brother was still good-looking. Hundreds of women must have shared the same opinion. Simone had tried to make subtle introductions, never succeeding. He had remarked on this, only to be attacked for having too much imagination, but he knew.

Simone had all the domestic comforts and security and wanted her brothers to have the same. She saw it all from a woman's point of view, never understanding how a man's mind worked. Her happiness stemmed from her whole personality. She was productive, not merely from the maternal aspect, but in contributing to the welfare of others. All except Karin. Simone had never tried to give Karin very much.

'Shall I pour?' Marc asked, reaching for the teapot. He had seen Leo move his hand as if to do the same.

'It's habit with me,' Leo apologised. 'No sugar.'

'I think there's a piece of stale cake.' Marc went to get up but Leo spoke quickly.

'No, don't bother. I'm not hungry.'

His eyes moved about the room to finally rest on the cupboards. He wondered what kind of larder his brother had. What would he find if he were to open any of the doors? Somehow, he could not imagine Marc living off baked beans and cornflakes. His thoughts interlinked and he began wondering about other cupboards. Marc dressed well. Did

47

he starve himself to keep thin or was it that he could not be bothered? Was he selfish, or mean, or both, or neither?

'Going back to our talk at lunch,' Marc said, interrupting his thoughts. 'I want to know if you're happy about things before I start talking shop. There are a couple of contracts to be signed and the new machines to be installed.'

'As long as you think I'm capable,' Leo said.

'Of course you are. You're quite capable of running that factory on your own. Blindfold if necessary.'

'Karin thinks I'm pretty useless. She's probably right.'

'What does Karin know about business?' Marc was angry.

'What does she know about anything except clothes and cosmetics?' Marc had never heard Leo talk about her before. He had protected his wife for a long time; making excuses for her, telling lies to himself. Now he spoke as if he knew that Marc was aware of this.

'Leo, you either have to tell me everything, or nothing at all. I don't want to pry. You could say it was none of my business, but it is when it affects other things. It's all related, unfortunately. I can't go off until I know that you can manage both work and your life. What are you going to do?'

'I don't know. What would you do?'

'You can't expect me to answer that,' Marc replied slowly, slightly shocked by the question. 'I don't know enough about these things.'

'Have you ever considered marrying?'

'Once I dreamt about it.'

'What happened to your dream?' Leo asked.

'Reality can sometimes change. For me, it became a nightmare.'

'I thought I could love her. I suppose you find that hard to understand?' Leo spoke with resignation.

'On the contrary,' Marc replied, 'I understand very well. You have to get things in perspective. Get your priorities right. Karin is in good hands and with treatment can be

48

cured. She isn't a true alcoholic. She needs understanding, sympathy and a great deal of love.'

'She's *had* all that.'

'No she hasn't. You've given her all the material things, but that isn't enough Leo. She needs you and she wants you.'

'I don't want her.' He looked up with slightly misty eyes. 'You don't understand, do you, Marc?' He shook his head. 'No, you couldn't possibly fully comprehend what I haven't the guts to admit.'

'You don't have to.' Marc replied. 'I've known for some time that it was not entirely her fault. And I admire her for sticking by you. That in itself surely must prove that she's loyal. In any relationship, if the need is there, the wanting is just a little way behind. We both know there are a lot of men who envy you for having such a talented wife.'

Leo leaned back in his chair and studied his brother with narrowed eyes. 'The Greeks called a piece of money a talent. Your use of that particular adjective is, I feel, very apt.' He sighed. 'She has been very expensive, but only because my conscience demanded that I make amends.'

'Self-pity won't get you anywhere.' Marc said. 'Whatever your desires and impulses are, they should not detract from your physical appearance. At least act like a man.' But Leo had forgotten he was a man. That he had to appear strong and resilient at all times no matter what the odds, or his inclinations. The veneer he had covered himself with suddenly dissolved, as if melted by the tears which trickled down his sallow cheeks to fall on the shiny surface of his brother's kitchen table.

Marc very quickly noticed how emotion had finally caught Leo. Seeing him like that produced mixed feelings; feelings of sadness, weariness, pain and frustration. Marc thought, watching him, that pity at that moment would be disastrous. He wanted to go to him and put a hand on the rounded shoulder, hoping it would give some sort of comfort, but the training he had received, just from the sheer experience of living and learning how to stay alive, made him check himself, caution being an embedded routine. All signs of emotion had gone out of the window, replaced by a silent anger.

'Pull yourself together! I'll get you a drink. If you want to wash your hands, the cloakroom is halfway down the hall.' He was grateful to have the excuse of getting the drink. The episode had not embarrassed him, but he knew that Leo must have felt a little awkward having finally weakened in front of him.

Leo found him in the drawing room and gratefully took the drink. Marc noticed the shaking hand in the late afternoon light.

'Sorry.'

Marc replaced the stopper in the decanter. 'Think nothing of it.'

'I feel lousy.' Leo stated.

'Tell you what, go upstairs and have a sleep. Later you can shave and shower and we'll go out to dinner. There's absolutely no need for you to go home tonight.'

'I don't want to put you to any trouble,' Leo mumbled into his glass.

'No trouble. Now that you're in charge, we must go over those contracts before I leave.'

'Yes.' Leo hesitated. 'By the way, when do you plan to set off?'

'Wednesday. The through flight to Marseilles.'

'Would you like me to drive you to the airport?'

'Yes, I would. I'd like that very much.'

'Would it be all right if I come over to Nuage too?'

'Of course. But not just yet, there's a lot to be done.'

'I could help you couldn't I?' Leo's words were offered as a plea.

'Leo, I shall need all the help I can get. Besides...' his face broke into a smile, 'If I remember correctly, you're a pretty handy man to have around, especially with inventive ideas.'

'When will it ... be?'

'Soon Leo, very soon. You can help with the grape harvest, and I don't mean sample the produce!'

'Thank you Marc. I'd best go home now. I'll phone in the morning. Goodnight!'

6

Marc slept during most of the flight, the free newspaper passed to him by an over-made-up air hostess remaining unopened on the spare seat next to him. Flying via Paris, the plane was only half-filled with passengers. There was the usual mixture of brilliantined business reps and clinically clean nuns, their starched habits almost creaking as they moved in their allocated seats.

More people boarded at Orly. He watched them through half-closed eyes, deciding that the hum of the plane's engines was more sleep-inducing than local chatter. He thought very little about Simone or Leo. Family thoughts had become filed away in the back of his mind. The problems could remain pending until his return. His mind did not want to work, for some strange reason, on what had happened during the past few days. That morning, he had begun to wonder if it really was only several days since Karin's accident and the complications arising from it.

When he took it all apart, he knew that, subconsciously, he had made his decision before this recent episode. That decision had been postponed, due to other commitments, but the final choice had been made ten years ago, when he had travelled in the same direction to the same destination, the family believing him to be in Paris on business. In a way, he was. Only a few of them knew of his previous visits. His odd trips were not secret, only his actual whereabouts. Even Simone's interest never went beyond enquiring whether he had enjoyed his few days in Paris. Charles occasionally gave him a knowing glance but never pursued the matter, and Leo seemed to ignore the whole thing. The family assumption was that he had a woman hidden away in a pleasant Paris apartment.

Charles once awkwardly suggested that prostitution in Paris could be expensive. The intimation was unacceptable for Simone, whose imagination would not stretch further than her vision of Notre Dame and the Pont Neuf in springtime. Her older brother was no saint, but his preferences were not the same as those of her younger brother, who was overtly gay. Whatever Marc did in Paris was his business.

The pilot announced that they would soon be landing at Marseilles. From the small window Marc saw the terrain, beautiful in its almost savage presentation. The backdrop of steep hills: green, purple and brown, falling down, surrounding flat-roofed houses of white, in the encroaching dusk, clinging to outcrops of rock, throwing shadows which were a welcome barrier against the heat during the day. Puffed-up clouds drifting over golden acres of corn, where ripening wheat met miles of lavender in bloom. Already he could smell what he knew was already there and always would be, a delicious mixture of perfume and colour; thyme, oregano and hyssop, interspersed with small outcrops of mountain savory and fennel.

The last time he had been at Marignane, there had been a muddle at immigration, due to an oversight of his not signing his new passport. It had been later in the year when he had arrived in warm sunshine. Now it was almost dark and, outside the terminal building, he felt the menacing fingers of the first chill of autumn as the Mistral clawed at his face. It reminded him of days and nights; the long interminable hours spent in strange places with other *resistants*, shivering from the bitter cold or suppressed excitement tinged with fear.

He stood by a tobacco kiosk, its shuttered windows sheltering him and, to a certain extent, hiding him from the harsh neon lighting inside the building he had left. Somehow, his eyes played little tricks. The leaves of the palm trees brushed against each other like silk against flesh. He smelt the strong aroma of burning black tobacco and then saw the small flame of a *briquet* shielded by indiscernible hands.

The flame moved and he saw the silhouette of a man's figure, standing on the other side of the entrance to the terminal. The head moved, the flame became extinguished and in the darkness a cigarette glowed red, its timing a little slower than the faulty strip-light, which attempted to flicker thirty metres away. The shape moved towards him until there was a short distance between them.

'Monsieur?'

He recognised the voice immediately. During dark nights, he had heard that same voice so many times, it was almost like hearing echoes of the past.

'Philippe!'

In his eagerness to embrace his employee, loyal family retainer and close friend, Marc tripped over the suitcase and would have fallen had Philippe not acted so swiftly. The man's arms shot out and grabbed him by the waist. Marc was then pulled to his feet. He felt the moustache on his cheek; smelt the aromatic tobacco mingled with garlic and wine. He took a deep breath. With a torn poster helplessly flapping behind them, they embraced, their final hug disturbed as the wind lifted the one remaining corner of the placard advertisement, ripping it from the shutter.

'Forgive me,' Philippe sniffed, running a finger down his cheek. 'You have to forgive an old man. Senility is a terrible thing, but I suppose if we remember that it starts from the day we are born, it isn't quite so shattering.'

'That's something you'll never be,' Marc said, bending down and picking up the case.

'What, old?'

'No my friend, senile.'

'Come,' Philippe said. 'I 'ave the chariot waiting, it is best that I drive. They have changed the streets and the traffic systems are as they were when the Boche altered them. It is all *sens unique*. Good flight?'

The ancient van had seen better days. Safely it had carried everything God and the Maquis had decided it should convey. What suspension it had whined and protested as Philippe pushed it to a speed almost beyond its endurance.

After Aix, he took the N296 and Marc knew they had nearly finished with the swerving and lurching he had forgotten about while living in England. He thought of the main roads with their monotonous impersonal directness and compared them with what he now felt around him. It was quiet and he could see little, yet he knew the surroundings.

Philippe changed gear and turned sharply up a narrow lane. Halfway, he changed gear again, muttering under his breath, 'I think it is time the estate had a new servant. This one has been a faithful one, now she should be retired, like me, a little rusty and slow in places.'

Marc held his tongue beneath his teeth. 'Are you trying to tell me something?' Had Philippe spent the last few years contemplating the remaining years of life as a free man with a pension? He must have done that during his time spent locked in a prison cell.

Marc realised that Philippe had not answered him. He let it go, knowing that if there was anything to be said, the bailiff would tell him and at the right moment. During his last visit, they had had almost the same conversation. They needed a new vehicle, especially with all the planned work on the chateau. The van reached the top of the hill, choking, gasping for air, then plunged down an even narrower lane towards the rusting ancient gates of the Chateau Nuage. The tyres chewed at the loose gravel, squealed a little and stopped.

'*Voila!*' Philippe remarked, getting out and slamming the van door, his voice carried away by the wind. He fumbled with a door key, twisting it in a lock stiff from lack of oil, until the door gave way and lazily swung open. He stood back, holding out a hand, silently ushering Marc into the large hall, which had once been Marc's mother's immaculate domain. The once exquisite mosaic tiled floor had long gone, as had the marble statues.

Philippe left him to take in the place. Everywhere, a smell of mustiness exuded. It was a mixture of damp, age and heat, all permeating from the woodwork, discarded furnishings and stone. Marc had smelt it before in many other places. It was the same atmosphere of death and decay, only now he stared at inanimate pieces of broken furniture and fallen stone instead of inert, crumpled, blooded bodies. It was an atmosphere of despair.

Philippe beckoned him. Marc stood for a moment longer before moving away, his footsteps loud on the filthy, blackened floor that his mother had ordered to be daily heavily polished by an army of servants.

The loyal bailiff had not wasted any time during the few moments he had spent in the kitchen. A large wooden table had been hastily cleared of rubbish and he was arranging two chairs to one side. In the hearth, obscuring the view of what had once been a beautiful fireplace, stood an old wood-burning stove, the glass door smashed long ago, disallowing any form of draught to enter its hot confines but permitting smoke to exit. A small pile of twigs was fighting to remain alight. Spirals of blue smoke curled from the broken glass door, slowly rising to play with the bare light bulb suspended from a long flex over the table. Marc watched him as he worked. Philippe was now sixty-seven years old, but as active as ever. He had changed little. It was the first opportunity that Marc had had of studying his face and figure, the hair still fine and grey, just as it had been when they had first met over thirty years before. He could not see the face clearly, as Philippe was adding more wood to the fire, but the scar on his left cheek remained, reminding both of them of one night in particular, a lifetime ago.

'I have bread, cheese and sardines,' Philippe announced, moving a chair and waiting for Marc to sit. 'Come.'

Marc took off his jacket and draped it over the back of the chair. He began to roll up his shirtsleeves, and then he undid his tie, placing it on top of the jacket.

'I think a little wine,' he said, getting up and going across the room. He stopped by another door.

'Mind the rats,' Philippe warned. 'I don't think there's a light, take my torch.'

With both hands, Marc felt the walls as he cautiously began to descend the stone steps. The open door above him allowed a shaft of light from the fire to guide him until he got to the first bend. Philippe's torch was flickering and useless. On a piece of stone, which protruded slightly from its original position, he saw a candle. Lighting it, the flickering dim glow followed him down into the depths of one of his father's beloved wine cellars. If his memory served him right, there were sixty such places.

During his last visit, he had only seen the outside of the house; he had not wished to go inside. No imagination was needed to tell him what he would see when he entered.

Standing at the bottom, he lowered the candle, steadying it on the top of a battered tin trunk, until it became embedded in its own grease. He kicked the dust beneath his feet, his shoes now thick with dried plaster. It was not the dust of thirty years ago; it was the detritus of centuries.

A large rat scuttled across the floor in front of him. He crossed to the other side of the cellar and saw the ancient wine racks. To his amazement, some spaces were filled, and he smiled. This was Philippe's way of announcing something without wishing to sound pretentious. Reaching out he selected a bottle, its label long gone. There was no point in wondering anything about it for the Germans had taken everything of value, especially the wine. Lovingly he stroked the cold glass neck; it was a moment he did not wish to share with anyone, not even Philippe. The last time anyone had done a similar thing could never have had the same resonance, he thought. After all, Nazi officers, even if they were high-ranking, knew nothing about wine. By comparison, German wine was almost undrinkable – after all France had the *terroir*.

He heard Philippe calling, retrieved the candle and hurried upstairs. The fire crackled and the smell of pine resin drifted throughout the room. Philippe had opened the sardines and was spreading them over ripe camembert on large chunks of bread.

'Are there any glasses?' Marc asked.

'No,' Philippe said, 'only mugs. This is not the Hotel le Louis Quinze.' He sighed. 'Ah, those were good days,' he reminisced.

Marc took the bottle to the enormous earthenware sink where he knocked the top against the edge. After checking the break was clean, he selected two mugs from a cupboard and filled them with the wine. A little surprised by Philippe's statement, he drank deeply from his mug.

'Are you serious?'

'Of course, we finally beat the bastard, did we not?'

'Eventually, yes, but at a terrible price. Was it all worth it?' Marc asked.

Philippe unscrewed a dead Gauloise cigarette from his bottom lip before he replied. 'I believe so and you do too. Ask yourself, why are you here now?'

Marc gave no reply, but thought about his reason. Was it national pride, inherited arrogance? 'There are things I need to know, Philippe, and you have the answers. You know why I'm here.'

As they ate and drank, he began to feel the warmth from the flames on his face and arms. Philippe had banked up the fire and switched off the light, now no longer needed.

'I think you should see Father Francis,' Philippe said. 'Even he does not know all of them. Perhaps you should go and see him tomorrow. I think you should.'

They sat on either side of the stove, their legs fully stretched, their conversation light, but always reminiscing. Philippe asked after Simone, and after Leo. He showed no surprise when Marc said that Simone had two children and that Leo was married.

Reaching in his trouser pocket, Marc pulled out a handkerchief, wiping his mouth and fingers. 'That was good,' he said. 'Now, a duty free cigar to help finish off the wine.'

Without answering, Philippe bent over a small pile of logs and fed the fire. The crackling wood disturbed the silence and an owl screeched outside, its call competing against the wind.

'You like the wine?' he asked, dusting off his hands.

'Yes,' Marc replied. 'Has it all been like this?'

'Mostly. You got my letter and the last reports?'

Marc nodded. The regular correspondence he received from the accountant, the lawyer and Philippe was his only contact with the estate. He relied on Philippe to manage the whole thing, as he had done since the disappearance of his father.

'Philippe...' he paused and drew on the cigar.

Philippe sensed apprehension. 'Something is wrong?'

'No, nothing is wrong. I only wanted to say that I believe we can make a start on the house. The vineyard has really been a huge success, a miracle after the Boche violated it and destroyed everything. I went over the accounts before I left.' He puffed again at the cigar. 'Yes, we can make a start.'

Philippe was quiet. He wanted to consider all the ideas and plans they had shared since those far-off days of hiding in the mountains and killing the enemy. They had shared a common dream; of rebuilding the Chateau Nuage and returning it to the grandeur it formerly possessed.

'You have enough money?'

'Ample. I want the estate to be self-supporting again. The

vineyards will expand, especially now that our application has been given the go-ahead by the authorities. Do you know, Philippe, I saw our wine with the Nuage label, on sale in London. I have given the whole thing considerable thought. Yes, it must be now.'

Philippe shifted in his chair. It was easy for his employer to talk about plans and possibly easier to think when away from a given situation. The estate had changed like many other things. The younger people were leaving the land their fathers had tilled, to find more money and more excitement in the cities and resorts. The truth was painful, yet how could he hurt this man who sat beside him? A man who was not only his employer but also his friend, who had twice saved his life. At one time they might have become related – Sylvie was his first granddaughter. In each of them, there existed a complete trust of the other.

However, there were things disconnected with the house and estate that bothered Philippe. His one wish was that Marc would eventually be told by someone else.

'The 800 hectares adjoining us.' He coughed. 'The land you suggested buying and adding to the estate, with south-facing slopes, good for vines.'

Marc sipped his wine, staring into the fire. 'What about it?'

'It's too late. Someone else has bought it.'

Marc looked across at him. The firelight made the scar more pronounced. 'Anyone I know?'

Philippe shook his head. 'I don't think so. He breeds wild boar and has people, mostly Americans, for hunting parties. I hear he makes a great deal of money.'

'I'd like to meet him,' Marc said.

Philippe poked the fire. 'You will, I've no doubt.'

Marc nodded. His jaw stretched in a yawn. The time had rushed by and, with all the talking, he had not realised how tired he was.

'I have a camp bed for you.' Philippe got out of the chair

and from beneath the table dragged out a folded bed. Tied to it were blankets and a pillow. 'I thought it best for you to sleep in here. Upstairs is very damp and not too clean. And,' he added, 'dangerous.'

'What about you?'

Philippe smiled. 'I have my own bed. I'll leave now. What time shall I return tomorrow?'

Marc squinted at the face of his watch. He yawned again. 'Not too early.' Not waiting for Philippe to take his leave, he began to undress.

Philippe pulled on his crumpled beret and went to the door. 'My granddaughter, Marie-Jeanne, will leave some eggs for your breakfast, but there isn't any ham.'

Marc smiled. 'Bacon,' he said. 'It's still as peculiar to me as it is to you. Goodnight, Philippe, and thank you.' He heard the squeak of Philippe's rubber-soled shoes, then the door closed and he was alone. As he fell on the bed in a state of half-collapse, the bed announced its sympathy and rocked unsteadily on its three legs.

7

Small cracks of light pushed their way through the shutters. He had slept soundly, dreamlessly, his bed comfortable in spite of being a little too small. Lying there, tracing cracks in the ceiling, he began to plan the day. Philippe would come, expecting him to make a tour of the vineyards. He did not want that yet. He wanted to walk where his fancy took him; noticing the changes, possibly making notes of the alterations he wished to make, wanting time to consider any modifications.

A noise outside made him sit up. He half rolled out of bed, his legs bent because the contraption was very low to the ground, and went over to the window. Opening it, he slipped the catch of the shutters, pushing them outwards, allowing the morning sunshine to burst into the room. Only when he touched the wall did he realise he was completely unclothed. He went to snatch his shirt from a chair when his attention was diverted by a movement outside. A girl, probably in her late teens, was walking away from the building.

She walked past a hedge, turned down the centre path of the neglected kitchen garden and headed towards a wicket gate in the wall. A basket swung freely in her hand. He watched her, the hair, fair and reaching beyond her shoulders, lifted as the wind touched it. He could not see her face.

Her hand reached out, pushing the latch with one quick movement, as if she were accustomed to doing the same thing daily. She turned to close the gate and then vanished behind another hedge.

Slowly, he began to dress. He lit the fire, boiled some water, but instead of washing and shaving, prepared a large pot of coffee. While waiting for it to brew, he went to the rear door. The bolts, stiff and rusty, were uncooperative, but he dipped a finger into the remnants of fish oil in the near-empty sardine can and applied it to the metalwork. Gradually he managed to slide the bolts across and stood in the soft light of morning, his eyes on the basket of eggs at his feet. They had small wisps of hay around them. Picking two up, he felt their warmth.

Philippe had said she was his granddaughter. Marc had imagined her to be a small child. What he had seen was quite different. Sylvie, a figure of his past, had become personified in her sister.

He lit a cigarette and smoked, contentedly. He sat and stared at the eggs; drinking too much coffee and smoking continuously, he waited for Philippe. He wanted to go outside, to breathe the fresh air and watch the sunrise over the hills, but he was afraid that he might see her again.

A soft whistling announced Philippe's arrival. Marc was rinsing his mug at the sink when the door opened.

'I've brought more wood,' Philippe said. 'How did you sleep?'

'Fine. Want coffee? I'm waiting for the water to boil so I can shave,' Marc apologised, rubbing his face.

Philippe laughed as he sat on the edge of the table. 'Like old times again,' he kindly said. 'Remember the beard you had?'

'Only too well,' Marc answered, drying the mug. 'Remember the lice in it?' He passed him a mug. 'Help yourself. I've had enough.'

Philippe saw the untouched eggs. He raised his eyebrows in surprise. 'You haven't eaten,' he said. 'She will be very upset if I tell her.'

'Who?' Marc tried to sound unconcerned.

'Marie-Jeanne. She came especially to leave them.'

Marc poured hot water in the sink and began lathering

his face. He noticed the softness of the water. He remembered it well. How easy it was to make bubbles when his mother or a nurse was bathing him.

'I'm sorry,' he apologised. 'You don't have to tell her. Now, what's our agenda for the day?' He continued shaving while Philippe gave him a fairly detailed plan. He allowed him to finish speaking and smiled in the cracked mirror. 'Philippe,' he said, still looking in the mirror, 'I want the morning to myself. There is such a lot I have to do, but I cannot begin to build the final picture until I've got the feel of the place again. You do understand, don't you?'

Philippe nodded. *'Bien sur.* You will see changes.' He lowered his voice. 'I thought I'd warn you.'

'What kind of changes?' Marc draped the towel round his neck and began combing his hair.

'Last time you were here,' Philippe began, 'it was a short visit. You saw few people. You never had time to understand what was going on.'

'Going on?' Marc faltered. 'No, I don't understand.'

'You will. All I ask is that you don't question me until later.'

There was silence. Philippe, slightly embarrassed, got up and moved away. He had achieved what he had set out to do, but now felt guilty. He knew it was his duty to be truthful, but he also felt his duty was to protect Marc.

'Come to my cottage when you are ready,' he offered. 'I'll wait.'

'Give me a few hours,' Marc replied quietly. 'I'll have a walk to the village and call in on my way back. I may drop in on Father Francis.'

'No!' Philippe's voice rang out. 'Please...' he hesitated, 'please do not go into the village alone. If you do, let me come with you.' Philippe pulled on his beret and hurriedly left, before Marc could question him further.

Slightly confused by Philippe's behaviour, Marc did not follow him immediately. Slowly he took himself off towards the vineyards. For Marc, they were an accepted sight, but for a stranger, they would have perhaps looked curious in their general appearance. Here, in the past, Van Gogh and Gauguin had drawn and painted such scenes with realistic accuracy. His vineyards would perhaps have caused Dali to leap with joy.

As he stared at the empty vines, their leaves turning copper and gold, he remembered they would soon be burnt, to invigorate the new shoots for next year. He walked between the rows, their wizened arms touching his knees, and he noticed they were beginning to sprout. Maybe Chateau Nuage would have a good year?

But Marc's mind was not concerned so much with what he saw or touched. It was desperately trying to reconstruct what had been said in the kitchen earlier. Something was wrong. Philippe was trying to spare him; he was an old friend and confidant, but he was still an estate employee. That, thought Marc, was the difference. Philippe had his duties to perform, and Marc as employer, had responsibilities.

Leaving the field, he followed a goat path, gradually climbing the hill beyond. At the top, he sat down. His fingers poked at the dry ground with a sharp stone. He noticed how easy it was to open the earth, to ease the dirt from its resting place. It was like the dry rot he had observed in the chateau on his arrival.

A sudden noise seemed to come from below in a plantation of trees. Birds, disturbed from their resting places, dispersed noisily around the apex of the taller oaks. The sound repeated itself as if someone had fired a rifle, one sharp crack and then silence. For a moment, it was as if he were back at Simone's, with the rooks crowing in her garden.

He was soon on his feet, searching for the owner of the gun. The oak trees were his, planted by his grandfather, as long as a century ago, and were to be used for renovations to the chateau. He could see the demarcation line, a natural ditch, the rocks covered with grass and scrub, dividing his land from his new neighbour's property.

Slightly alarmed, he began to climb down the other side of the hill. It was difficult to stop his legs from breaking into a run. His feet slithered against the grass and he turned them inwards in a braking action.

When he reached the bottom of the valley, he was hot and breathless. He could see nothing out of the ordinary. Walking quickly, he took a dirt track that the goats had mapped out, skirting the trees, and on reaching the other side he saw a tumbledown farmhouse.

Was he trespassing? His intentions were innocent but the shots intrigued him. There were several abandoned homesteads in the area, mindlessly destroyed, lying neglected like the chateau, and he did not wish to be accused of prying. For one second, he wondered if the farmhouse was his property. He turned round to check and saw the tell-tale ditch now behind him in the distance.

The house was empty. He saw the damaged front door, blistered by a relentless sun. There was no sign of life. He walked round to the back, studying the structure. Tiles were missing from the eaves, although the higher ones shone brilliantly from the slight film of dew on them. An open window in the roof clung precariously to a solitary hinge, the metal imprisoning a faded piece of material, which he assumed had once been a curtain.

A few brown hens scratched at the base of a muck heap. They ignored him, quite content to rake over the fly-infested straw, rotting in the sun. He crept to the nearest glassless window and peered in. There were obvious signs that the place was inhabited. The furniture was scrappy and dilapidated. Flies swarmed around a half-eaten loaf on the table, the lower part saturated by wine which had spilled from an overturned bottle. What had once been an inviting wheel of camembert cheese now oozed pale creamy fat from its seams.

His thoughts went back to Karin. They kept going back to her, a fact he found disconcerting, and now he wondered how things were in England. He walked away, his anger beginning to grow. Obviously, the cottage was a tenant's, maybe belonging to his new neighbour. Were his own in a similar disgusting condition? He felt a weight in his stomach at the thought.

The whole atmosphere, the dreadful picture of poverty, neglect and bitter ugliness, was like a canker. He had a dream, a hope that had dwelt within him for a long time, a wish that he wanted to fulfil. As he climbed the hill again, he kicked viciously at the loose stones. It was his fault, his cowardice and pride had not simply spoilt things: his total and irrevocable guilt of gross neglect had changed his dream into a hideous nightmare.

Marc was not entirely to blame. It had been the enemy occupiers who had brought the disease, and he watched it spread like fire across his world, his birthright, his personal domain. His initial reaction was to go directly to the village. Only Philippe's words stopped him. Philippe was wise and intelligent. Unlike most of the local inhabitants, he had received the benefit of a good education through the benevolence of Marc's father who, realising his potential, had encouraged Philippe to accept the offer of a chance to better himself. The old man knew that Philippe was capable of managing the estate the way he wanted it run. Above all, Philippe was cautious. The warning he had given Marc had been sincere, his tone forbidding.

Marc made his way back towards the lane. A man working on an enclosed patch of scrub eyed him suspiciously. When Marc waved, the peasant picked up a hoe and turned away, a defiant gesture of contempt.

The lane twisted in front of him, cutting its way through clusters of rock. He stopped, wondering whether to rest or go on. As he decided to continue, the sound of voices came from behind the next outcrop. He stopped, leant against a rock and waited, curious to see who was walking in the opposite direction.

Two men and a dog appeared. One man was holding a rifle in the crook of his right arm, the other, much younger, a mere youth, was speaking in rapid German and, on hearing him, a shudder went through Marc.

He remained where he was, waiting for them to look up. The younger man saw him first, muttered something to his companion, and they quickened their pace until they were level with him. Steel blue eyes, their stare penetrating, pierced both his own. Marc returned the gaze, noticing the man's large square face, the grey hair with its low parting, and the tight mouth. A strange stab of déjà vu possessed his mind. He met so many men like this in business and in prison.

'Hans Grich,' the man bowed slightly, 'and if I'm correct, you must be Marc Chevaud, my neighbour.' He turned, faintly touching the other man's arm. 'And this is my nephew, Rudi. We are just on our way back to the house. I'd be honoured if you would join us for a drink.'

Did the German really live in the pigsty of a cottage? Marc studied the gun, his observation so intense that Grich spoke again.

'I see you are interested in the rifle. It only arrived this morning and we have been trying it out. The sight needs some adjustment, but on the whole I am pleased with its performance.'

'It's a very fine piece,' Marc said. 'I heard you when I was walking in the wood. You gave me quite a scare.'

Grich smiled, gold fillings noticeable against the whiteness of the other perfect teeth. 'I apologise, and if you would accept my invitation, I could perhaps show you that I mean it. After all, we are neighbours and neighbours should be hospitable towards each other.'

Marc looked at his watch. He was torn between what to

do. The stranger was a smooth talker with a slick Teutonic tongue. His mistrust of the race as a whole was deeply rooted. If Grich was his neighbour, then he wanted to know as much as possible about him. But he was also anxious to learn about other things. It was necessary to keep his priorities in order of importance. Grich could wait until later. Only one person could help him. Philippe Coutanche, a wily old peasant, whom he respected and trusted, and for whom he would die.

'I'm afraid I can't this morning,' Marc apologised. 'I have duties to attend to in the village. May I contact you in two or three days and invite myself over?'

'Of course.' Grich moved his rifle into a more comfortable position and turned to Rudi. 'But we have no telephone as yet. Come,' he said to Rudi, 'before the sun gets too hot for you.'

They began to walk away and Marc raised a hand as they reached the next group of rocks. As soon as they had turned the bend in the road, he thrust his hands in his pockets and began walking in the other direction, with only his fears to accompany him.

8

A small collection of sparrows perched along the top of the low wall dividing the churchyard from the lane, leading down to the village. Undisturbed, they continued their noisy chatter, taking no notice of him. The church had not changed at all apart from certain features that had either disappeared or had been defaced. As Marc reached the lych-gate, he met a woman coming the other way. She finished crossing herself, looked at him disdainfully, and then hurriedly crossed herself again.

Once inside the building, he automatically dipped a finger in the cold water in the font and made the sign of the Cross. A life-size statue of the Virgin Mary gazed fixedly at him. Her placid smile conveyed no silent message. The man-made expression had no calming effect on his body or soul.

He took his time walking down the aisle. He had probably travelled along these flagstones a thousand times in the past. As a small child, he had regularly attended mass and communion three times a week, with his parents and, later, Leo. Simone had only been there once, to attend her baptism.

The faith meant nothing to them now. Marc had lost his beliefs long ago in his attempt to understand the futility and distastefulness of war. Leo appeared faithless, and Simone, more English than the average Anglo Saxon, had become an Anglican.

Yesterday, the sun had shone and he had glowed from within. Now the yellow ball was still there, high in the heavens, but the warmth had gone. He felt cold and empty, yet simultaneously full. It was an odd sensation, this acceptance of truth. Perhaps it would have been better if he had been told all the facts. Why would Philippe have warned him in such peremptory tones not to go into the village? It was his village and he was the Seigneur. He assumed he had now succeeded to his father's title, making him a Comte. No! He was still a man, a changed man, cynical and angry.

The truth was as clear as the white paint on the church walls, pockmarked with bullet holes. He was guilty of neglect. He had deserted his people, leaving them to work on an estate they served because there was nothing else left. If they refused to labour for the Germans, imprisonment and death were inevitable. His people shared his dreams. They failed in hope as he did. Behind his back, they accused him of cowardice. Running away, abandoning them to a dreadful, unbelievable fate, and for many of them, ultimately death. Only God could forgive him and them for their wrongful conclusions. He had suffered beatings and torture yet he was still alive. At times, he wished he had not survived.

His thoughts went out across the miles to Leo. How would he have coped in a similar situation? It was difficult to know if his younger brother had hidden depths.

He had given these people nothing. He was nothing. At least in the eyes of his tenants he was a nebulous character, taking them for granted and expecting hard labour for very little reward. How could they respect him? They did not even know him.

In the family pew, he knelt on the hard floor and buried his head in his hands. A few candles burned; evidence of earlier that morning when the small church had accepted those seeking consolation from its spiritual atmosphere and relating to the priest an account of all their wrongdoings.

He did not hear the footsteps, only the voice. It was soft, yet there was a strong resonant tone about it, the deep nasal dialect and patois of the south.

'I'm waiting, my son.'

71

Marc gradually lowered his hands. He stared ahead but knew he would see nothing. He did not have to search. The voice had not changed. All he needed was a little time to collect himself while raising his body to its full height before entering the confessional.

On the custom-made seat, he tried to sit without being too close to the grille. He could not bear the thought of having his face against the fine wire mesh. It was too reminiscent of a Gestapo cell he had once occupied. There was no need to whisper. He had no secrets, his alleged crime was public knowledge. Just a few, besides the Almighty, knew the whole truth.

'*Monsieur le Curé*,' he began, immediately regretting his opening remark.

'Marcus, does an absence of a few years mean we have to be on formal terms?'

Marc closed his eyes. 'Father Francis, I do not want your forgiveness. I need your help.'

'Is this just another fleeting visit?'

The words were not said sarcastically but they hurt. Marc released his clenched hands. He slid to the floor and knelt as best he could in the tiny box that smelt of age, camphor and incense, his elbows resting on the seat of the chair, his feet uncomfortably pressed against the closed door.

'Bless me father, for I have sinned. My last confession was...' he faltered. He could not remember. The last time he had seen the parish priest it had been a social occasion. He felt the pressure of his hands against his face, nails digging into his forehead, the cupped palms pushing the flesh of his cheeks into his eyes, forcing them to close.

'I'm sorry,' he said. 'It's no use. I can't go on.'

There was a silence until he heard the creak of another door. He waited, then heard the light hollow tap on wood. He obeyed the signal and, a little ashamed, left the confessional box.

A beam of light pierced the damaged stained-glass window, its slanting ray finally resting on the first seat of the pew he had used moments before. The priest stood, his body bowed a little, on the first step in front of the altar, facing the Host. Marc observed with compassion the faded black robe, its uneven hem allowing the heels of worn-out shoes to show against the patched strip of the threadbare carpet.

'Coutanche has told you?' the priest enquired without turning.

Marc sat down. 'No,' he said. 'What is it he has to tell me that I do not already know? I know what I have done.'

'That is the tragedy. You have done nothing.' The old man moved backwards, bowed his head reverently, and then slid his way into the pew. Marc studied his profile. The skin was rapidly falling into folds of loosely-knit flesh. The man had not changed inside and never would. He had taught Marc responsibilities, rights and moral duties, and now he thought his pupil had failed him.

'Father Francis, if you could speak to them. Explain to them why I had to remain in England. I did not totally desert them. I came back here whenever I could. You above all know that. Coutanche has worked miracles in the vineyards, but he could never have done it without their help. Now there is enough money to rebuild the estate. Don't you see, Father?' He took a deep breath. 'Do I mean that little to them? How can they hate a stranger?'

Father Francis lifted a hand and dropped it with resignation on Marc's knee. Marc saw the brown pigmentation of advancing years and the swollen knuckles, the protruding veins, resembling mountains looking down on a network of blue streams and rivers.

'My son, you are confused and you have reason to be.' He half turned, patted the knee he was touching, then once more clasped his hands together. 'After what you have suffered, naturally, you would think like this. You believe the people

73

are angry because you went away and they assumed you had left them. You believe they think you have taken them for granted; exploited them as they laboured to keep alive something which, I suppose, might be termed an anachronism.' He paused. 'Isn't that so?'

Marc slowly nodded his head. The estate was a thing of the past. Perhaps all the material things it contained had outlived any usefulness. Only the soil remained.

'Marcus, I have to tell you something which is going to pain you very greatly.'

'Father?'

The old man edged his way from the pew and stood resting in the aisle with one hand on Marc's shoulder. 'Come, the Almighty will give us just as much courage outside.'

An elderly woman, heavily dressed in black, stood waiting to enter the porch. She gazed at Marc with eyes filled with pity. He felt her sorrow, surprised that it was not anger. He held the door for her, allowing her to pass. When he had closed the door, he could smell the perfume from the flames of the candles intermingled with incense.

With silent steps, he followed his companion along the path. The priest, a little breathless, stopped to rest by a large shrub.

'I keep forgetting,' he apologised. 'There used to be a seat here. Like most other things, the Germans took it away; they wanted the iron to build more tanks.' He coughed. 'My old bones won't allow me to sit upon the grass. They even took the metal which surrounded the graves.'

'There is the wall,' Marc replied, and left him to follow until they reached the stone barrier. Marc heaved himself up and sat, his legs dangling loosely against the stones. Father Francis remained standing, leaning heavily on the granite. Marc could not see him clearly; the sun was too bright and he had no dark glasses. But the priest could see him and he thought of two crucifixions. The one he had not seen had

74

been symbolic and physically cruel, yet the one he was witnessing at this moment was a mental one. It was difficult differentiating between self-pity and disappointment. Which one disturbed his lost parishioner?

'I'm ready,' Marc said, quietly. 'Don't spare me. I want to know everything.'

'I wish I could spare you.' Father Francis pushed his hands in his pockets and stared at his shoes. 'I had hoped Philippe would tell you.' He sighed. 'When I have told you, you will understand why he could not do so.'

From the pocket of his shirt, Marc took a packet of cigarettes and lit one. The smoke hardly moved in the stillness, until it touched the brim of the priest's cappello hat.

'Your people, and remember, they are yours, should be happy that you have returned, but they are not. You automatically believe it is due to your neglect of them.' He paused. 'It isn't. In fact, their attitude is based on a hatred that has grown instead of diminishing. Time is a meaningless thing out here. It is measured by the harvests and the ever-changing colour of the earth. One would think that after twenty odd years, their memories would fade a little. Regrettably it has not happened.'

Marc smoked in silence. All those years! Where had he been at that time? Area Twelve or was it Area Ten? His memory was certainly fading. Of course! He was there hiding in the well house for months at a time. Obeying orders direct from London.

'But some of those people were not even born!' he protested.

'Cast your mind back,' the priest replied. 'Not to your own activities, but to those of this village.'

Marc reflected. He was met with blankness. The priest moved against the wall, his shoulders stiff.

'You have no idea, have you?' The question was expressed with compunction.

Marc shook his head.

'It was no different in the beginning,' the priest said. 'The village was the same. The people slept safely in their beds, continued to work and live as they had done for decades. Even when the Germans arrived, it stayed the same on the surface. They commandeered the estate, put high ranking Nazi officers in your father's house, filled it with badly wounded men, and I must admit, ruled us almost tolerably well. Few women were raped.' Marc immediately thought of Sylvie. 'Some men were sent off to labour in German factories. In the beginning, we even had sufficient food. They did not often get drunk in public and they were attentive to our children and your wine stocks.' He stopped uncertain how to go on. 'That is until the villagers discovered the truth.'

'Truth?' Marc wished the old man would get to the point. At the same time, he felt sorry for him; almost understanding how difficult it was for the priest to speak at all.

'There is an English picture, I believe,' Father Francis continued. 'A famous one of children being questioned by soldiers of Cromwell.' He paused. 'I would ask of you the same question, my son.'

'You know when I last saw my father,' Marc began. 'You were there at the quay with the rest of us, waiting for the boat. I remember you gave Leo a medallion. That was the last time.'

'I wish I could say the same, but I cannot lie to you as you do to me. Your father had a pact with the enemy.' He could not continue. Marc watched the old man's face, twisted in anguish. He saw the lips quiver, and the Adam's apple slide up and down when the priest attempted to swallow.

'My father is dead.' Marc said, his words final with a sign of acceptance. 'I know.'

'Yes, he is dead,' the priest's voice was very low, the words barely audible. 'The men of the village accepted that he was a collaborator.'

Marc slid from the wall and stood rigid from shock. His

first reaction was to take the man by the shoulders and to shake him. He wanted to jerk him so violently that the ill-fitting false teeth would slip down the throat and choke the owner. He clenched his hands, his teeth, and felt the blood pounding in his ears.

'If you weren't a priest – my father? Never! I won't accept that. It is you that should know the truth. My father was an agent for the British.'

Father Francis slipped a hand from his cassock and took Marc's stiffened arm. 'Anger is an emotion that I understand. I, too, felt the same, but because of my cloth, I had to suppress it. I had to release it by kneeling on the cold stone floor of the church for twenty-four hours. I was taken away, beaten and locked in a cell – guilty of showing a light from the candle I had lit. They said I was signalling the enemy. I don't know if I achieved anything from my actions. I doubt it, but at least I prayed for his soul. I prayed for all of you. A few, a very small few, knew what was going on.'

'You have proof?' Marc said, his hand shaking as he lit another cigarette. 'I want proof, Father. Proof.'

'The villagers' attitude now, isn't that sufficient evidence? You still have contacts in London. They know.'

'No!' Marc said loudly. He looked across the lane to the far side. 'I want you to tell me, and when you have finished, I will go to Coutanche and ask him for verification.'

'As you wish,' the priest said. 'Philippe has buried his anger over the death of his granddaughter. The men responsible for her murder were all mutilated by the local Maquis. You know of that, you were involved. When it became known what your men had done, ten hostages were taken from here and publicly executed in the square. Benoit Constantine's brother was decapitated and Remy's.'

They stood, their shoulders touching. The priest could feel Marc's body trembling from anger and shock.

'The factory in Toulon. The Germans took it over. I believe

it was an engineering works – we were never told. A few men left here to work there, your father's doing, I suppose. They continued to produce components, but they changed the type – it was something to do with aircraft. As the owner, your father knew in 1938 – even then he was a Nazi sympathiser, like thousands of others who believed in the regime speeches and empty promises delivered by a madman. In our blindness and stupidity, being such simple people, we thought we owed our freedom and our ability to go on as we had done to the fact that the Germans were deferential to your father.' He paused. 'We, of course, were losing the respect we had for him. They needed your father; his brains and his factory, it was good propaganda. We were a model village of occupation. Even the Maquis behaved and concentrated on targets miles away, but of course, you know all about that.'

'How did he die?' Marc asked, flicking the cigarette stub through the air and watching it as it fell to the ground to smoulder. He was reacting in the same way as if he had been tossed in the air, and had fallen to the ground, still burning. He began searching the names on the tombs nearest to him.

'I'm surprised you do not know,' Father Francis said. 'Didn't London tell you? He was working in the factory when Toulon suffered the heaviest raid in the war. It was he who signalled to the allied bombers with a flashing light.'

'Do you mean he wanted to be killed?'

'Possibly, your dear Papa had lost the will to live. I imagine he was burnt to death or blown to pieces. You can search the whole graveyard, he is not here. Had we looked for his body, it would never have been found.'

'So he was never buried?'

'Ask Coutanche,' the old man said, walking away.

'But...' Marc ran after him. 'Why do they blame me? I knew nothing about that. Surely they knew where I was and what I was doing – for them, for France. Philippe or you could have explained.'

'They know nothing, my son. Philippe never speaks of the war, not to us. The people only remember events that occurred here, a long time ago. See that long line of crosses over there?' He pointed. 'There are always fresh flowers on them. Count them. Killed because of what you did to the soldiers who murdered Sylvie. That was the price we paid. From the moment those ten young people were murdered, we were no longer a model village. We were as stiff and cold and lifeless as the corpses we buried. Many of the people have remained that way.'

By the door of the church Father Francis stopped and turned to Marc. 'Now go to Philippe Coutanche, and tell him I forgive him, just as I hope the others will eventually forgive themselves for what they have thought. It is not a case of "like father, like son". Go in peace, Marc.'

Marc left him abruptly, but the peace the priest had hopefully suggested he should obtain was lost in a mind tormented by words he knew to be the hateful truth. His father had been a double agent and was certainly no traitor. The harsh glare of the sun cut his eyes to pieces and his head throbbed.

At first, he was unaware of his surroundings. He no longer cared where he was or where he went. When he saw the river, he felt he had come to the end. Was that the answer? To hurl himself into the water and pray he would sink?

When he reached the river bank he fell down, his legs seemed to fold beneath him. With both hands clasped around his stomach, he rolled and writhed in agony as he vomited, his body crushing the muted blades of green beneath his weight. Tears began to run down his cheeks and when the nausea had gone, he began to sob, his cries lost in the deepness of his own soil.

There was only one witness to his misery and torment. Marie-Jeanne crouched behind some rocks, her large canvas bag of provisions scattered about her feet. She had never seen a man cry. The sight of him did not frighten her. It moved her beyond all description. How could anyone like that be anything but good? She remained there, hidden, respecting his desire to be alone, until he picked himself up and washed his face in the clear, cold water of the river. As he bent down, she hastily collected her shopping and crept away.

Recently she had started to sing on her way to and from the village. She had good reason to be happy for she was in love. She wondered if Rudi ever cried. It was difficult to imagine. Yet it would have been impossible to think of Marc Chevaud in such a distressed state of mind, had she not witnessed it for herself. Her feelings for Rudi she kept to herself. Her knowledge that her grandfather hated all Germans warned her to keep her thoughts and feelings locked inside. On her way back to the village, she was silent.

9

The old kitchen had become a living room in every sense. Marc thought how incongruous the neatly-made camp bed seemed amid the nakedness of the light bulb, the smoking stove and the dripping tap. He compared the things he saw: his umbrella, a symbol of Anglicised convention, standing in a corner with the ancient pump, which guarded the chipped porcelain sink, like a sentry half-asleep with sloped rifle.

Philippe too thought it strange, as he watched Marc from the other side of the room. Marc Chevaud, now so typically English on the surface, in his city uniform with rolled umbrella. Once it had been a Sten gun and primed grenades. Now, he deduced, his surroundings would be an office with a deep leather chair, a large imposing desk and an attractive secretary, who perhaps helped release other pressures besides official ones. The only ammunition his employer would use in his realm of industry would be his brain. His life on the other side of the Channel was another world, exclusive, remote and totally private. The enormous financial hand-outs Marc had given had unquestionably helped the estate, but Philippe usually spoke with cautious scepticism, convinced that Marc could obtain anything he wanted.

From his general appearance, Philippe knew that Marc must have sought a confrontation with the priest. The afternoon shadows growing longer were still no excuse for the face he thoughtfully studied. It conveyed an expression of tormented sadness he had frequently seen during the war. But in those far-off days, war was not necessarily a purely personal thing. Most men had lost the art of laughing, their minds too full of revenge and bitterness, bordering on hatred.

'You asked me to come to your house when I was ready,' Marc suddenly spoke.

'And you are not. I can wait,' Philippe declared.

'How long? Another twenty years?'

Philippe winced. He had tried to protect a man he loved and respected. He had wanted to spare him more pain. They had shared love for Sylvie, his beloved granddaughter. Over the years, he had secretly dreaded this day, but the yielding of the past and all its rotten truth and stark realities had arrived. He had pushed his loathing away, but now it was with them, horribly alive.

Marc got out of the chair. 'I need a drink,' he stated.

Philippe shook his head. 'You need a little warm milk and plenty of sleep. Brandy is too stimulating at a time like this.'

'How would you know about time?' Marc angrily pushed the chair out of the way. 'That's the whole point of my coming back. To build...' He put up both hands, spreading the fingers. 'Twenty prolonged years of work, plans, ideas and hope. Months of thinking ahead in order to get all this back to what it was. Now...' he paused. 'Now, there seems little reason for keeping the place. I have made a decision, Philippe.'

He stopped, aware of his bitter outburst. His anger had not faded since his meeting with Father Francis. Walking in the fields had not completely released him of the rage he thought would rip him open. The despair of Sylvie's dreadful fate added anguish to his fury.

No longer did he wish to see anything, not even the face of his closest friend. He closed his eyes, but the blackness was filled with strange symbols. There was no way out of the forest. He thought again. It was not a forest, more a wilderness, bare, bleak and vast. He was drowning in his depression and no longer accepted feelings of hope and ideas of any kind of future.

Did man create his own wilderness or was it placed before him to allow scope for manoeuvre? Was he to use his life in an almost vain attempt to cross that plain of isolation? What did he do when he arrived at the much sought-after well? Drink deeply, or spit the water from his mouth because it tasted impure? Or did he ignore it because it was pure and he himself was unclean?

He was alone, a solitary figure conscious of his failings, his failures, and above all his weaknesses. He had built on an idea and in his desire to succeed, had become over-ambitious. At times, his plans were reaching the realms of the impossible. He tugged at the door of the cellar.

'No,' Philippe said, moving closer. 'Cognac will do you no good.'

'Go home, Philippe.' The words were final.

'I'm sorry,' Philippe whispered.

'For what you have done?' Marc replied, pulling at the door.

'No,' Philippe said, his right hand coming down on Marc's neck. 'For what I am doing now.' He caught him as he fell against the door. He remembered what they had been taught, but he had not taken his age into consideration. Marc's body was heavy and he had difficulty dragging it across the floor. It was harder pushing him on to the bed. He was glad it was not his own high, brass-railed frame, reluctantly inherited so many years ago from a sentimental mother.

Tenderly, he covered Marc with a blanket. Then he crept to the other side of the room, switched off the light and settled his aching body into a chair. He did not sleep continually. Marc was ill. The truth had been staring him in the face for ages. Mental illness was probably the worst of diseases. It was misunderstood, showed no visible symptoms, like lumps or scars. His employer was fighting for survival with bouts of guilt.

Philippe sat up with a jolt when he heard the shot. It was

nothing new to hear the sound but he had never been aware of any firing at such an early hour. He swore, looked at Marc's body as it moved beneath the blanket, and then cursed again. The hatred he felt for Hans Grich was daily growing into something too great for him to accept as a natural emotion. The last thing he wanted was to have Marc disturbed. It was too late.

Philippe pulled open the windows, then threw back the shutters. The tempting lifting tone of daybreak lightened the trees with a softness he associated with the land he loved and to which he belonged. His eyes scanned the view he knew so well, the picture being completed by the smell of good rich earth. Away in the far distance, he saw the mountains, their snow-capped peaks pink from the reflection of a rising sun. For a moment, he forgot Hans Grich.

This was his Provence, where the land blended a wild ruggedness with softened beauty and the people were as strong and as independent as the soil at which they worked. Unsophisticated, occasionally referred to as indolent, they were friendly and genuine, their carefree ways innocently emitting a magnetic charm of its own. Turning away, he saw Marc standing by the unlit stove.

'I'm cold,' Marc said, rubbing his arms. 'Is there any wood?'

Philippe nodded and began raking the bottom of the stove until it was free from ash. He filled it with twigs, struck a match and waited for the flames to catch. In ten minutes they had a good fire, providing enough heat to boil a pan of water.

'There's no milk until Marie-Jeanne arrives,' Philippe said. 'Do you mind having black coffee?'

'It isn't a case of minding.' Marc put a hand to the back of his head. 'I think "need" would be a better way of putting it. What did you hit me with? An axe?'

'Just my hand,' Philippe replied.

Marc pulled off his shirt. He tossed it onto a chair and

went to the sink. 'Thanks,' he muttered, gripping the pump handle.

'She should be here soon,' Philippe said, watching him. 'I was hoping you would sleep for another couple of hours. Someone will have to stop him.'

'Who?' Marc asked, his head beneath the running water.

'Grich,' Philippe answered, picking up a towel and throwing it across the room.

'I didn't tell you,' Marc said, drying his hair. 'I met him yesterday with his nephew. They were trying out a new rifle. It was one of those latest Spanish high-velocity models. Pretty good stuff. I thought he was quite pleasant. In fact, I liked him and the nephew.'

'I was afraid you would,' Philippe mumbled and moved away.

Marc draped the towel over the edge of the sink. He opened his suitcase, chose a shirt. All the time he was thinking about the gun. The hostile remarks made by Philippe had not gone unnoticed. Philippe's aggression and open dislike of all Germans might be excused on the grounds of what he had suffered, but they had all suffered in different ways.

'You said he hunted boar,' Marc stated. 'Does he have a licence?'

Philippe shrugged his shoulders. 'I do not know what he does.' Philippe was about to say more when the handle of the door rattled. He unlocked it and pulled it open. Marc finished buttoning his shirt. The girl remained on the step, a basket on her arm and a loaf beneath it.

'*Grandpère*.' She kissed Philippe affectionately, put the basket down and passed him the bread.

Philippe looked at Marc. 'My granddaughter,' he said, 'Marie-Jeanne, this is Monsieur Marc.'

For a moment, Marc forgot himself. His granddaughter – Sylvie's sister! It wasn't possible. Philippe's wife and daughter-in-law were dead, dying of illness brought on by malnutrition, like so many others. Their son had been conscripted by the Germans, to work down the mines, and eventually died of silicosis. Thankfully, Philippe spoke positively of his liaison with one of the few women left in the village when he needed comfort and reassurance.

Marc could only think of how he had dreamed and almost convinced himself that he was losing his sanity by clinging to delusions. His mind went backwards, working on the memories of the morning before, when he had watched her opening the gate. Then, her face had been obscured. Now it was there, a real face, full of life and exquisite innocence. The large blue eyes smiled beneath the flaxen hair.

'Monsieur,' she whispered, lowering her eyes to stare at a floor covered in dust, particles of sticks and scraps of paper. He realised as soon as she spoke that she had misunderstood his silence. Inadvertently he had embarrassed her. He held out his hand and she immediately looked up at Philippe, as if silently asking what she should do. Philippe nodded and she felt Marc's hand on hers in a brief clasp.

None of them spoke. She made the coffee, cut the bread and emptied the basket of food. Philippe, intent on eating, ignored her, but Marc found he could not take his eyes from her. Every movement, every gesture, forced him to concentrate on her presence. When she had finished, she went to his chair, her hands reaching for the dirty shirt he had thrown over the back. He leaned forward and she pulled the shirt away.

'Excuse me, monsieur.' Shyly she backed away, wondering if she had done the right thing. This man was a legend to her. Only once had she seen him as close. She had been ten years old. Her birthday! They had given her a tea party and later she had played with the other children in the village square, trying to catch the doves, which frantically fought for scraps of cake. Marc, who had been in France in 1955 on a business trip and had made a brief detour to Nuage and, walking across the street with Philippe and the priest, had stopped to give her a coin.

Now she remembered the recent time when she had seen him. Her recollections of the previous afternoon were disturbing. It was difficult to know why he had wept. It could not have been from unhappiness. He was a rich and powerful man and would have many friends. She looked at him again before going to the door. He was the sort of man who felt deeply about things. He must have wept from nostalgia or pain, she thought, gathering the towel in her arms and rolling it up with the shirt.

'I have left enough for your midday meal,' she said. 'I will come back and prepare supper at six.'

She kissed Philippe quickly, and went to leave, but he put out a hand, his grip forcing her to remain by his chair.

'And why the hurry?' he asked, looking at her suspiciously. 'These days you are always in a hurry. Where are you going?'

'To wash m'sieur's shirt,' she replied, 'and clean our house.'

'All day to clean out a small house?' Philippe questioned. 'Don't you mean Monsieur Grich's camper van as well?'

'*Grandpére*, you are hurting me,' she whispered.

He released her and she almost ran from the room before he could say any more.

Several moments lapsed after she had gone before he spoke again.

'Her looks and her figure make many problems,' he sighed.

'Problems for you or her?' Marc asked.

'Both,' Philippe said. 'You know what it's like. You must have had it with M'selle Simone. They are a responsibility these young girls. Besides, I don't want her having too much freedom. She will marry whom I say and when the time is right.'

The dogmatic reasoning stunned Marc. How would someone like Philippe ever come to terms with a changing world? The so-called liberation of women had gone a long way, but he doubted its power in a place where marriages were still arranged over a game of boules and a bottle of good wine.

Marc rose from his chair, strode across to Philippe and slapped him on the shoulder.

'You old devil,' Marc said, trying to laugh. 'How old is she?'

'Twenty-one in two weeks.' Philippe felt the hand still resting on his shoulder. As he spoke, he did not move. 'Do you think of her much?'

'Who?'

'Why, Sylvie of course.'

'Every day of my life, as I am sure you do.'

'Yes, Marie-Jeanne is a reincarnation of Sylvie, her dead sister.'

'It is incredible that an old buzzard like you can be blessed with two beautiful granddaughters,' Marc reflected.

'Their mother, my daughter-in-law, was so distressed over Sylvie's death and the aftermath. Thankfully, she was able to have another beauty that cheers us all.'

'Congratulations,' Marc said sarcastically, wondering, how did Philippe's son manage that?

'We should make a pilgrimage to Sylvie's memorial.'

'Of course, whenever you say.'

'We are friends again?'

'Have we ever been anything else?' Marc replied, pushing across the table a packet of Gauloise the girl had thoughtfully brought. 'You know we have to talk?'

Philippe nodded, took a cigarette and pushed it between his lips. 'I am ready,' he said, accepting a light. The flame momentarily illuminated the scar. Marc, before he had time to realise what he was doing, put two fingers on the other man's face.

'Does it hurt?' he asked, quietly.

'No,' Philippe said, taking Marc's hand and indicating that he understood. 'Only the memories.'

Marc pushed the cigarettes and lighter into his shirt pocket. 'Let's go outside,' he suggested, pulling at the door. 'We can make a tour at the same time. I want to see everything. Especially the new vines you planted last year.'

As Philippe followed him though the wicket gate at the bottom of the neglected kitchen garden, he only had one question to ask. 'Do you think you will stay?' he queried, squinting, as the smoke of the cigarette painfully stung at his eyes.

'It all depends,' Marc replied, heading for the first outbuilding he could see.

They were both hot and tired when they returned to the house after two hours of walking round the estate, followed by another two hours jolting the ancient van along tracks unfit for anything more than horse-drawn carts. In four hours, they had seen only one other human being, the postman; dark, lean and short of breath, struggling up the hill. Marc had watched him as the man stopped for a while to rest against a rock, noticing how he emptied his cheap leather shoes of the small stones collected during his long climb. Then, when on more level ground, he remounted his bicycle and rode off, crossing himself as he passed a wayside shrine.

Marc had hoped Philippe would end the tour by driving into the village, but he took the higher road and hardly spoke on the return journey, following their visit to Sylvie's memorial, in the sanctuary of the forest.

With the cold chicken Marie-Jeanne had left, they sat on the top step of the veranda, both too hungry to continue their discussion until their stomachs were full. The red wine was deep and full-bodied and they washed down the meal with long pulls at the bottle.

Marc wiped his fingers on the single napkin that had been wrapped around the chicken and then passed it to Philippe.

He leaned back against the stone balustrade, lit a cigarette and sighed.

'Are you content?' Philippe asked.

'Not really,' Marc said, playing with the lighter. 'Would you be?'

'No, I would be as you are, worried, sad and very confused. You have seen the vineyards and all the other living parts. What about the house and the decay?'

'What do you want me to say, Philippe? That I put every penny I have into something I want to believe in but can't?'

'It is your decision,' Philippe murmured. 'Just tell me when you have made up your mind.'

'I can tell you now,' Marc said, looking across the courtyard and hoping that Marie-Jeanne would appear. 'I'm going through with it because I have to. I'm going to take the bastards for every franc I can squeeze out of their secret Swiss bank accounts.' He stubbed out the cigarette, put his hands behind his head and gazed up at the cloudless sky. He heard a sniff and tactfully waited while Philippe blew his nose.

'You emotional old frog,' he said, still staring upwards. 'You know, I've worried about the factory, my brother, my sister and this place for too long.'

'And all at the expense of your health, no doubt,' Philippe said.

'Perhaps,' Marc muttered. 'I never had much time to think about myself except to acknowledge the loneliness.'

'You should have a woman.'

Marc shook his head. 'That's not enough for me. There is more to love than that. I do not want anything. But there are certain things I need.' He stopped, remembering that he had used the same words when talking to Leo. Then he thought of Karin.

'All right! You still need a woman,' Philippe answered.

'Yesterday was just about the end, or so I thought,' Marc continued. 'But that is all over. I've done too much thinking.

From now, we stop dwelling in the past. We are going from day to day, until we can be reasonably certain of the future. We cannot change yesterday.'

'If I am a frog, then what are you?' Philippe asked, his face beginning to crinkle in a half smile.

'Me?' Marc shifted on the step. 'I was a philanthropic snail. I made my shell and crawled into it, when I wasn't trying to organise the rest of my family.' He gave Philippe a quick glance. 'I've only just realised that the two gastronomic nouns I used are both symbolic of France.'

'And both highly prized,' Philippe added, getting up and stretching his arms. 'Now that we have done most of the physical survey work, when do you want to go over the accounts and check the books?'

'Tomorrow will do.'

'I'll come back this evening,' Philippe suggested. 'Then you can explain what you are going to do to the chateau.'

'Yes.' Marc rose to his feet. 'After yesterday, I have to get back to the people. I've got to help them. Somehow I've got to let them see that I too have to forget, and forgive, although I don't know how we can ever forgive a dead man.'

'That's a priest's job,' Philippe mumbled.

'Is it? I wonder. I hope they realise that what I intend doing will benefit everyone. With all that is about to happen, they'll soon forget the past and start looking ahead.'

'Not a pleasant proposition for everyone,' Philippe said, disconsolately. 'The future for some of us includes old age and ultimate death.'

'That,' Marc replied, walking away, 'regrettably, affects us all.'

Philippe limped off in the opposite direction, annoyed that he had allowed a few lightly-spoken words to aggravate his fears so acutely. The aggravation simmered enough to remain in his already troubled mind for the rest of the day, his normal duties undertaken with less attentiveness than usual.

It was a little too easy for men like Marc and Hans Grich, he concluded later that evening, as he limped home. They took or bought what they wanted. He frowned when he thought of his granddaughter; could she be bought too?

As he drank his Pernod alone, there was murder in his heart.

10

Marc was alone at last, in the rambling emptiness of the house. As a chateau, it was small, but to him, as he strolled through the ghostlike building, it was immense. All at once, he realised he had disproved a theory; that children think of things as enormous and on seeing them again, as adults, are amazed that they are really quite small.

Wandering from the salon, he found the library and suddenly all the childhood memories that occupied his tormented thoughts flooded back. He found it difficult to accept the room as he saw it; his mind imprinted with flashbacks of his father seated at a table, reading. Now, there were no books. Even the shelves, on which the numerous collections had been lovingly placed, had disappeared. Between the long, glassless windows he examined the niches, the marble, chipped by unappreciative visitors, rough on his fingers. Once, the two alcoves had been filled with magnificent floral displays created by the Comtesse. That was the only time his mother had been allowed to visit the room.

It was going to be a tremendous task, he decided, drawing the double doors together – the beautiful, ornate doorknobs had gone, leaving gaping holes. The expense did not matter, but would there be enough time? He was concerned that the enormity of the project would overtake him with age. He was still deliberating as he hurried to the *toilette turque* to relieve himself. The wine over lunch/supper had been too much. In his haste to pull down his zip, he jerked a little too hard. He stood, trying to repair it, reminding himself to tell Leo that they should modify their latest design, before

93

considering a contract with a large trouser manufacturer. Eventually he gave up, leaving the two giant iron footrests to keep vigil each side of the hole in the floor. He wanted fresher air than the odorous atmosphere he had been forced, by nature, to suffer.

The staircase, with its rococo panelling, was larger than he remembered. At the bottom, he craned his neck and looked up at the chipped plaster. The boards were bare and dry with no lustre of polish to catch the eye. He went up with hesitant steps, dreading any further havoc he knew he would inevitably find.

On the landing, he came to the first door. It swung open easily, revealing more bare boards and curtainless windows. The dirty panes of glass gave an impression of haze falling on the untidy drive below. The bedroom was empty apart from one huge wardrobe in a corner. Shutting the door, he tried the next one.

Even before he had fully opened it, he knew something was amiss. He stood motionless on the threshold staring at the figure of Marie-Jeanne. She swung round, the vase she was holding dropping to the floor with a resounding crash. Gasping, she bent down to collect the pieces around her feet. Although several metres from her, he could not fail to notice her trembling hands, clumsy in their attempt to retrieve the fragments of china.

He walked across to where she knelt and stood looking down on her. She managed to move her fingers in between his shoes, dusty from all the walking he had done. Then she looked up, terrified of what she might see. To her astonishment, there was no anger on his face.

'What are you doing here?' he asked, very quietly.

'I meant no harm, m'sieur.'

'What are you doing?'

He patiently waited for her reply.

'I am sorry,' she said, getting to her feet. 'I meant no harm.'

He kicked out with one foot, scattering the remaining bits of porcelain across the floor, until they hit the skirting board or fell between the gaps in the floorboards.

'*Grandpère* will be waiting.' She backed away, as if paying homage to a dignitary.

Marc did not move.

At the door, she turned and said, 'M'sieur, you are not angry with me?'

'No.'

'*Grandpère* would be angry if he knew.'

'He will not know,' Marc said, realising that she was leaving, and hurriedly joining her. 'It can be our secret.'

'I have not told him yet about Rudi,' she said.

Following her downstairs, he took care to remain at a distance for fear of releasing his one desire to touch her, his wish merely to prove that she was real.

As they reached the bottom, Marc touched her wrist. 'Please, tell me more about Rudi.' He felt a strong need to protect her and was curious to know more about the Germans.

'Yes,' she said, her voice eager. 'Yes, and I can make you some English tea.' She laughed, showing straight, even teeth. 'There is tea. *Grandpère* likes tea.'

He let go of her wrist and joined in her laughter, although his own was a little forced. 'Very well! You can make the tea and I will listen while you pour.'

She ran ahead to the kitchen and began to rummage in a cupboard, taking out an old tin containing tea, and two rather fine cups. As she busied herself, he watched, perfectly content and happy that he was going to share a few moments with her. He went to sit and she ran forward, her arms held out.

'The laundry!' she exclaimed. 'I have washed your shirt and the towel.' She took them and placed them on the table. He nodded gratefully and she went back to the stove. If only he had known how she had washed the shirt; carefully and with delicacy, because of the fineness and the quality; terrified of spoiling it.

'Tell me about Rudi,' he said, as she passed him the tea.

'We come here, sometimes, when it is dark.'

Astonished, Marc put down the cup. 'You come here at night?'

'Not really, but I have been here in the late afternoon. I had to wait until Rudi left.' She stopped. 'Otherwise, we would have been seen. Now his uncle knows and I go to their camper van twice a week.'

'What do you do?'

Her face flushed. She picked up the tin of tea and replaced it in the cupboard. 'Talk and make plans.'

'Marie-Jeanne, how long have you been doing this?'

'Eight months.' She smiled at him. 'The tea is not good?' she questioned, going to take the cup.

'It is very good, but too hot.' He lied, not wishing to hurt her feelings. It was cold. Why couldn't they boil the water?

She picked up the old leather bag. He noticed the simplicity of her white overall, tunic-style over a pale blue dress. The slender legs were tanned and smooth. The clumsy sandals did not detract from the pretty feet.

'M'sieur, I must go. I have put food in the cupboard.' She left and he allowed her fifteen minutes before making any move.

The bailiff's cottage was half a kilometre from the village. It stood back in detached isolation from the lane, with a few cypress trees protecting it from the sudden temperamental gusts of wind that blew down from the mountains.

Marc ran across the garden and banged on the bright blue door. Seconds later, Philippe let him in, his face slightly pink. Marc was undecided on whether the colour was from over-exertion or embarrassment. Inside, he waited while Philippe slipped on his jacket.

'I was about to come,' he said, taking his beret from its hook behind the door.

'Sit down, Philippe!' Marc tried to be calm but his words still hinted at a command. 'It's got to stop, you know.'

'M'sieur?' The eyebrows were raised as Philippe answered.

'All this protectiveness.' Marc went to the window, his mind searching for the right words. 'I'm fed up with being virtually imprisoned in my own home. It's always the same. You come to me. You tell your granddaughter to bring food. We've spent hours and hours in that damned kitchen.'

'You have only been in France for a few days,' the bewildered man replied.

'And I have seen and heard all that I want. You thought you were helping me, didn't you? You thought that by coming to the chateau you were keeping me away from the village.' He turned. 'Don't think I am ungrateful, but I'm right, aren't I?'

'Yes.'

'Now tell me why.'

Marc sat down and Philippe did the same. They each made their own personal calculations – Marc wondering what there was to know and Philippe uncertain of what his employer had been told.

'Where shall I start?'

'Don't you know? I told Father Francis that I would have you verify all he told me.'

While listening to Philippe, Marc occasionally got up and walked the length of the room before sitting down again. It was almost dark and, from the window, he could see the odd light from an isolated house in a distant valley, flickering against the blackness of the sky and the shadows of the mountains. When Philippe had finished, he watched him shuffle away to return with an oil lamp.

'Is that everything?' Marc asked.

'Everything you were told by the priest.'

'But not all?'

'There is more, but will it help?' Philippe pulled down the glass funnel on the lamp and regulated the wick. 'Please try to understand,' he went on. 'The Boche were trying to get away with as much loot as possible before the Allies arrived. There was no law, no order. It was hell let loose. They were so jumpy, they became more trigger-happy.'

'If my father was a friend of the Nazis, why didn't they bury him?'

'Because he wasn't here!' Philippe exclaimed. 'Your father was blown to bits in Toulon. He was no further use to them, they knew they were defeated. Their own skins were more important.'

Marc suddenly felt very weary. He stretched, then leaned forward in the chair. 'Now, tell me about Herr Grich.'

Philippe undid the buttons of his jacket, sat astride a kitchen chair and rested his hands across the back.

'Hans Wilhelm Grich,' he began, 'born 1918, a little older than you, of respectable middle-class parents in Hanover. Graduated from Heidelberg with a first-class degree, athletic, keen on flying. Hess was a family friend until he took off for Scotland. Arrogant, ruthless and maybe as wealthy as you.'

'Is that all?' Marc frowned. 'How do you know all this?'

Philippe ran his fingers along the back of a chair. 'Not quite,' he said. 'You see, Grich and I are no strangers. He possibly doesn't recollect me, but I remember him. He has been here before in the guise of a tourist. Possibly retracing some of his father's footsteps. Looking at the graves like the rest of them. I keep close contact with old friends in Paris who work for Simon Wiesenthal, the Nazi-hunter. Grich is a dangerous man, take great care!'

Marc considered he was doing the same, stepping back in time, looking for the truth.

'Perhaps if we begin on the books?' Philippe suggested. 'I've got some very good cognac.' He fetched the bottle and poured Marc a measure into a glass.

'Before we start on the accounts,' Marc said, 'I'd like you to write down a few things we have to do.' He drank the cognac and refilled his glass. 'After this excellent brandy, I may not remember very much.'

He waited while the bailiff took out a pen, then tore a leaf from one of the ledgers.

'One,' Marc stated. 'Have a telephone installed at the chateau by the end of the week. I shall need it and can't possibly work without one. Two, remind me to send telegrams to my brother and sister, telling them I'll be back next Saturday. Three, get a message to all the villagers and tenants that I would like to see them in the Bar des Pêcheurs at six-thirty tomorrow evening.'

He saw the look on Philippe's face.

'Don't worry, they don't have to talk to me. I only want them to listen. After all, they have a right to know what's going on. I can explain to them about their compensation still due from the German government. That should make them happy.'

'Germans are not known for their generosity!' Philippe complained.

'We'll see,' Marc said.

'Anything else?'

'Yes, I would like the van tomorrow. I intend driving to Marseilles. I shall leave early and be back in time for the meeting.' Marc pulled himself to his feet and went across to the large *vaisselier*. He saw a faded photograph of Philippe's parents and another of his wife. Philippe's eyes followed him. He could feel them on his back, but he did not ask any questions. Respecting Philippe's reticence about anything concerning his private life, he moved away. 'Give me the keys to the van,' he said.

Philippe took a key ring from a nail at the side of the dresser. 'Shall I come with you or walk over later?' he asked.

'You're coming with me,' Marc said, 'but we aren't going back to Nuage.' Outside in the darkness he called, 'Come on!'

Philippe shrugged his shoulders and mumbled to himself while locking the door of the cottage. 'Where are we going?' he asked, getting into the van.

'To Beaucaire.' Marc turned the key and heard the engine fire.

'Beaucaire?' Astonished, Philippe could not suppress his surprise.

Marc smiled, knowing that his companion could not see his amusement. 'Yes, we're going to walk through those streets of tatty old houses, and finish by having dinner in the best restaurant we can find.'

Philippe wondered if Marc really knew what he was doing. He had, after all, received several shocks in a very small space of time. There would be more, but they would have to be released at a more carefully chosen moment. A man, even if he were Marc Chevaud, could only take so much.

11

1941, Mont Valérien Prison

A true fanatical Nazi, Hans's father had lived, acted and obeyed each order given. As a German Major in the Waffen-SS, he was part of the great invincible army serving Hitler.

Fraternisation was a serious offence. If a soldier wanted a woman, he had to make use of a registered prostitute in an official brothel and pay the stipulated fees as laid down in a long list of regulations. The occupying forces took more than their pound of flesh, his own behaviour no disappointment. He well remembered his first encounter with a whore. During his first posting to Hamburg, celebrating his promotion to Oberst, he visited a sordid room in the Reeperbahn, with the help of some drunken comrades.

Oberst Frie was not just a quiet passive professor of art respected by many; he was also an ardent Nazi, always keeping his opinions secret, his orders strict. As a teenager, Hans had concluded that his father had a schizophrenic personality. Frie had held an official position at Mont Valérien prison, and by 1941 was proud of the fact that under his jurisdiction, 4,500 people had been executed.

Grich was not Hans's real name, but the maiden name of his mother. There were numerous reasons as to why he had done this. The official name on his birth certificate was Frie, but this became almost as notorious as had Quisling in Norway, and the name of Frie was remembered with fearful hate in the village of Mirabeau.

To keep the peace in the middle-class home, with its

puritanical and clinical atmosphere, Hans thought university would soften his father's attitude, and help him avoid further confrontations. Hans had changed his choice of studies from philosophy to European history. His mother, as always, remained tactfully in the background, not entering the argument, for fear of her husband's physical strength.

In his final year of studies, Hans received the greatest disappointment of his life. A directive came from his head tutor that only members of the Hitler Youth could be considered for a degree. His tutor, along with other professors, mysteriously disappeared. Most wondered where they had gone. One did not have to be of the Jewish faith to be marched away. Intellectuals were renowned for their communist commitments.

His father, Gunther, now a *Gauleiter*, had been made a Commandant by accepting a God's gift of a posting, taken when German High Command had requisitioned the imposing Chateau Nuage. The dispossession of the elegant ancestral home of le Comte de Chevaud's ownership was achieved swiftly and with typical Germanic efficiency.

The posting was a stroke of good luck. Gunther revelled in the luxury of grand living, secretly admiring the Louis Quinze chairs with burning jealousy. Miraculously, the paintings in their gilt frames were still intact. They were not in their positions for long as pillaging was rife. The Comte saw that they were swiftly packed away and crated, hidden in a secret place among the sixty cellars (some minute, others large with vaulted ceilings) in Nuage. Most of the antique furniture was locked away in the Comte's private apartments on the second floor. Later, the art treasures were re-hidden in a disused still room for safety. Philippe had a key and helped to pack them with loving care. The Boche could have the fake pictures hanging in the hall with pleasure.

New tenants rapidly filled the spacious rooms with iron beds and biscuit mattresses, on which wounded or sick men lay dying. Many of them clasped the iron cross to their breasts, as a devout Catholic would clutch a rosary, while incoherently muttering prayers.

Hans's father had been dutiful and regularly posted cards and pictures of the medieval village, lost for centuries in Provence, to his wife and children. His letters were filled with vivid descriptions of a magical place with a castle and soldiers guarding it. There was no beautiful princess; the handsome prince had run away to England.

Gunther, always searching to relieve a sense of boredom, had a deep yearning for not just a pretty face. His need for an interesting body was intense. These were in plentiful supply, as there was, in the majority of towns and villages in France, an acute shortage of men. Most of them had been sent to work in Germany or to camps in Poland. Women outnumbered men by five to one. Many of them were understandably hostile, even to gifts of Swiss chocolate or luxury silk stockings. He found it hard to ignore the drab, ubiquitous, cheap white ankle socks, most of which had become grey due to lack of soap for washing. The people wore wooden-soled shoes now as the order of the day, as the Germans had taken all the leather available for the Wehrmacht. Even Paris could be boring, as entertainment was banned or tainted by Germanic influence; the dreadful warehouses locked and filled with crates of stolen art treasures all destined for Hermann Göring's special train.

'Miracles' Marc refused to accept as possibilities. Certain business ventures had proved successful, giving him financial strength and confidence. During his short time in England, he had set up the factory with his father's financial help, and landed a government contract supplying zips for military uniforms. Now he was incarcerated in a French prison, which was controlled and supervised by the SS and German war veterans of World War I, acting in the absence of the Polish women who were delegated to perform the most menial tasks. On a July morning, the rattling of keys disturbed the shallow sleep he had finally snatched. Uniformed SS men stood in the doorway. Neither of them made any movement, but remained staring at him and speaking to each other in their native tongue. At a loss and feeling mild panic, which played havoc with his empty stomach, he remained motionless. Was this to be the end of the Chevaud dynasty – execution in the yard outside by firing squad?

'Well,' the heavy-jowled Corporal sneered. 'Don't you want to leave us?'

'You've got a nice comfy cell here,' the other one said.

'Of course,' the Corporal added, 'we have many vacancies. Get your stuff ready, we've got other things to do and can't waste time.'

He had few things to pack. The contents were hardly worth taking. Surprised, he walked with his two guards, one on either side, no handcuffs, and he thought how incongruous it must have looked, as they were impeccably dressed, wearing highly polished boots, whereas he was in filthy rags and bare-footed.

The door was the last one in a long corridor, lit by low-wattage wall lamps. He noticed there were no shadows and no windows. They came to a halt and the Corporal knocked on a metal door. For a moment, Marc thought he was being moved to another cell. Once inside, he saw the new surroundings. Were it not for the potbellied stove giving out an oppressive heat, he might have been standing in a large refrigerator. Everywhere was white, except for the menacing green door. A utilitarian desk and chair of bleached pine stood at one end of the room; there were no other chairs and no carpet, simply a single rug covering a metre of black and white tiles. In a corner, there was a large filing cabinet.

A man, also in the uniform of a Major, sat behind the desk, smoking a large cigar. He made no attempt to introduce himself. It was all a scene, a drama that had to be acted out, Marc surmised. The Gestapo were well practised in the art of interrogation. The purpose of the silence was humiliating intimidation of the prisoner, to bring him down to basics, to impress on him who was in charge, to summon tears.

Marc made no movement as the seated officer dismissed the two guards with the wave of a hand and then continued to read the document before him. Marc had suffered similar treatment before and thought he knew what would happen. He was in for a great shock.

'Sit down.' The Major spoke in fluent French. Marc's eyes searched for an absent chair.

'Oh, I do apologise, they have left them outside.' Shouting orders in German, the Corporal then returned, carrying a folding chair.

'No doubt you are wondering why you have been brought here?'

Slowly Marc shook his head. 'No sir.' He was grovelling, he hated his words.

'You may be interested to hear you have friends in high places M'sieur.' The Major placed the document on the file. 'I have here a permit ordering me to release you and for you to return to your home. That is for you and another, a M'sieur Coutanche.'

In disbelief, Marc closed his eyes; he didn't have a home to return to. 'When am I to leave?' he asked.

'As soon as you have signed this,' the Major tapped the file.

'By whose authority?'

'Of course,' came the quick reply, ignoring the question, 'you will need fresh clothes and a pass signed by me. You are free to go. Perhaps another time, we shall meet in surroundings that are more convivial.'

Not on your life, Marc thought. For an instant, he wanted to shake the man's hand and was tempted to proffer his own.

That was the trouble with the Boche, and the SS in particular – they were two-faced. This could all be a trick. Perhaps he would find himself re-arrested once outside the heavily guarded gates. To his amazement there was a car waiting outside, to take him and Philippe back to the village. Only Philippe knew Marc was in France. Philippe remained at Nuage, faithfully serving Marc's father and thriving on being a highly active member of the Maquis.

Mirabeau was not a large village, but in the twentieth century it remained medieval to the point of being feudal. Marc's father and his grandfathers before him had supervised the running of the commune, quietly, fairly and, in many cases, generously. Their name was held in high esteem, and respect was as indigenous as the mountains and great rivers Provence possessed.

The arrival of the Germans in convoys, men armed to the teeth and even the odd tank, brought gossip and suspicion, and smug smiles to the tan crinkled faces of men who toiled in the fields, spitting on wine labels before sticking them on bottles. They were confident the occupation would not be permanent.

The mayor had led a delegation to discuss the problem with the Comte who, to relieve the sense of loss of freedom, and to placate those whose tempers were beginning to reach danger level, remained calm and explained why he had sent his wife and children to London. For their health, he explained ironically.

His own problems were monumental, yet he had no one with whom he could share his ever-growing worries, apart from Philippe. Most of his tenants and workers were of peasant extraction, and many could not read or write. They bred like rabbits and he spent vast sums of money enlarging their cottages, to make room for more children, which arrived regularly.

The vineyards made a profit, but they did not make him

rich. His alternative business was a giant engineering factory in Toulon, producing parts for aeroplanes, and it was this which made him suggest to his eldest son and heir that he take an engineering degree at university. As the war dragged on, Nuage became another arm of Germany. His sixty-odd years had taught him how to be devious, astute in business. Against his will and reasoning, he decided to deal with the situation himself.

Official trips abroad were made, to neutral Switzerland, Portugal, Sweden and Spain, a perfect cover for many things. He made a deal with the Germans, not exactly a gentleman's agreement, as Gunther Frie was no gentleman. Michel Geoffroi, the Comte de Mirabeau, had no choice but to agree with the orders he was given, that the chateau, like so many large houses, was to be occupied by wounded Germans and turned into a hospital for sick and dying men, most of them repatriated from the Russian front, many with frostbite. In return, the Comte asked that the chateau be treated with respect and careful management. On occasions when talking to the enemy, he could be gullible. He believed their slick words, whereas his people did not. The slyness of the peasant was stronger than the cunning of the aristocrat.

12

Late 1943, Nuage

An angry winter had arrived with arctic ferocity and, like the many thousands of French people, Marc was depressed and had thoughts of returning to London. He had no news of his father, nor his mother. She was now living in a flat somewhere across the Channel, with Leo and Simone at school during the week. It was common knowledge that the war was in its final stages. The Allies were regularly bombing German cities by day and night. In France, hundreds were killed by Allied bombs. Toulon and his father's engineering works were destroyed by American bombers, which flew daily with impunity across the Channel, a thousand at a time.

There was talk of a second front opening and further imminent invasion. There was talk of many things, whispered gossip was rife while Paris became noticeably quiet, empty of the dreaded street patrols with their vicious dogs. Philippe and Marc talked about the forthcoming summer in the hope of a bountiful harvest of grapes, not that they gained financially from any wine produced as the estate worked for the Third Reich. Both men were occupied with the inevitable departure and farewells Marc would have to make.

The evacuation began and Nuage became a scene of organised chaos. Lines of trucks and ambulances lined the sweeping drive, many ignoring the gravel, and were driving across what had once been immaculately kept lawns. Stretcher-bearers were carrying the sick and wounded. SS officers were speedily running with armfuls of files and papers, to destroy them on an ever-burning fire.

Marc was well hidden in a semi-derelict well-house, several hundred yards from the chateau and camouflaged by the Maquisards, using thick bushes of flowering shrubs; spreading broom that ran rampant with wild tangles of honeysuckle and ivy. He had lost count of the time he had spent here, surveying his family home and German movements, watching troops and forever looking for his father. London had been tight-lipped over where the Comte was. They knew, of course, he thought they knew, or at least he hoped they did. During the latter years, there had been too much subterfuge, too many lies, too much pain, followed by intense anger, which was still burning inside many.

Marc had managed to survive through Philippe's pretence of him being a simple French peasant. Because of his clever play-acting, sadly, to the German troops, he had become a joke. Marc knew how much Philippe enjoyed this unforgivable taunting – as if he were on a stage, he would repeat comical gestures, taking curtain calls for an appreciative audience, but he had to be careful not to go too far, as mentally retarded people were sent to the gas chambers en masse.

Sylvie had been with him when the Morse key message was being tapped out. He finished his cheese-covered cold potatoes, wiping his fingers on his shirt, and signalled to her that he had to send an answer, once he had decoded the signal. She was aware that her grandfather and his employer were involved with the Resistance and longed to help in a small way.

'I must leave now,' she said grudgingly, '*Grandpère* asked me to shut up the rabbit cages.' She kissed the top of his head and let herself out of the shed. The message from London had told him of an uprising in Paris. 'Expect a large drop of arms, next 24 hours. Give assistance as soon as possible.'

'Idiots!' he exclaimed, pulling off the headphones. A tap on the door and he turned to greet his second-in-command, Remy. 'They have no idea of what's going on.'

'What news?' he asked eagerly. Remy sat down. 'Paris is a mess, there are tanks and Boche everywhere. What do we do now?'

'We carry on. We must get Daniel's group and all he can find to help. Go and tell the rest to be ready by seven, as dusk comes, and to bring every bit of ammo they can get hold of. We're going to need it.' He stopped abruptly when Remy held up a hand.

'What?' Marc asked.

'Didn't you hear that scream?' Remy urgently whispered.

'It's only a vixen at the quarry, she's been yelling all week.'

Once more Remy held up a hand, 'Listen,' he insisted.

Marc heard the screaming. 'That's no fox,' he said. 'It's a woman.'

His immediate thoughts were that Sylvie had left only ten minutes before. Desperately he reached for a knife in his belt and picked up a gun from the old box he used as a table. Changing his mind, he replaced the pistol and made for the door.

'Hurry, I believe it's Sylvie Coutanche. Come on!' he shouted. It was not difficult to pinpoint her position from the cries for help. In later years, he recalled two sounds, one of screaming, in her cries for help, '*Laissez-moi, s'il vous plait!*' and one of laughter from lecherous drunken German soldiers.

By now, they had been joined by a dozen Maquisards, all from Mirabeau and known to him. Instinctively, they all snake-crawled across the damp grass, using trees and shrubs for cover. The Germans had made their task simple by lighting a small fire, a rare mistake, which could have warned a stray Allied plane of their position. The enemy had become blasé, as if they wanted to be caught and have the hostilities ended. Had they any idea of the fate that Marc had planned for

110

them? Their laughter, turning to cries of beseeching would be as loud as Sylvie's screams.

The fire helped them to see in the enveloping darkness. The Germans had tied her to a large tree and in turn were raping her. When they had finished, the acting leader took a bottle from his pocket and poured the contents over her. His next act was to set light to her clothes.

Unable to speak through shock and disgust, Marc signalled to Remy that they should take each one of the six Germans. 'I'll see to Sylvie. No guns, just use your knives and no killing. Tie them to the trees, there will be coils of rope in their haversacks.'

Remy crawled away. Marc ran towards Sylvie, his knife ready in his sweating hand. Her torturers were expertly taken with heavy blows to the backs of their necks. Marc dragged a German's body away, fumbling for some rope in his pockets. Making certain his prisoner was secure, he ran to Sylvie and, undoing his flies, he urinated over the flames of her dress. Moaning, she collapsed in his arms and died. The sadistic attack was too much for her fragile body. Marc began to sob.

Between them, they carried her charred, broken body away. Marc did not join the others; he ran through the woods, tripping over roots of trees, their branches tearing his face and leaves, blinding him in the darkness. Light would be no help, as his copious tears created a salty mist over his eyes. It was imperative that he warn Philippe of the terrible events of the evening.

Philippe's dog gave a friendly bark and came running down the path. Behind him was his master. Marc's employee crashed into him, almost knocking him down. It was another kind of yell cutting through the darkness. The sky intermittently lit up by flares and flashes of explosions going on all around. Marc's own sounds came out as garbled hysterical cries, his muttered words incoherent, speaking of anger, revenge, hatred, of every conceivable thing, including his disbelief in God. Philippe, now also in a state of shock, guided him inside the cottage, and left him to weep alone in the kitchen. Marc's only comforter was a brown shaggy dog, which never tired of licking his hands, while he wished they would stop trembling.

13

1966, Return to England

On that afternoon, it was different. Simone felt a sense of apprehension. The feeling was evasive and it annoyed her. A crisis was about to occur yet it had nothing to do with Charles and his emergency meeting that morning. Later, after his arrival home and over his usual pre-dinner drink, she knew he would discuss it. He always did talk about everything. It was Marc! She knew it and felt it, but it remained a nagging doubt.

She had tried to dismiss it. The disagreement she and Charles had thrown themselves into earlier that day was probably the cause of her growing tension. She was alone, her solitude as stark as Karin's, but Karin could always talk to her psychiatrist. Simone had Marc for such kindness when difficulties arose. Now, she had no big brother in whom she could confide. Her guardian had flown off to France.

She missed the boys, especially Crispin. Piers had been in danger of becoming spoiled through over-indulgence on her part. When the dangers had become known to her, she had stopped being over-protective. Before Crispin had been born, she and Charles had discussed all the things young and inexperienced couples tended to talk of. Crisp was no longer a little boy squirting water from a toy pistol over his father or Uncle Marc. Piers would be joining Crispin soon at boarding school and then she would have even more time on her hands. It would rush past at a frightening speed. She would be lonely like Karin, becoming redundant to a certain extent, and boredom would enter her life.

Her thoughts became a little emotional. She replaced the cup in its saucer, threw the remaining cake crumbs to the waiting birds, and hurried into the house.

A small bowl of African violets whispered to her on the hall table. Piers had presented them on Mothering Sunday. She touched the vivid blueness of the petals. They immediately brought back thoughts of Marc. She and Charles had spent their honeymoon in the South of France, in the spring of 1955, when she was just eighteen. She remembered the evergreen foliage of the olive trees with a carpet of violets growing beneath them. They had seen green, blue and gold; the goldenness, an aura they themselves created from sheer happiness. Somehow, it had always remained.

She contemplated the dreams they had woven as she prepared tea for Piers. Now they had facts and reality, and when those were combined, dreams were inevitably scattered, becoming abstract in form.

On the day of Marc's return to England and expected arrival home, Simone visited Karin. She purposely avoided telling her that he was flying back that morning.

Karin was dressed, wearing the slightest trace of make-up. Simone noticed how well her sister-in-law was looking. The puffiness beneath the eyes had gone, the face was less drawn and the skin was clear. She had also lost a considerable amount of weight, which she could ill afford to lose.

Before Simone left, they chatted light-heartedly for an hour. Her short stay and hurried departure were noticed by Karin, and she found herself wishing her visitor would stay for longer. Simone was going to Marc's flat, but had no intention of telling anyone. It was going to be another brief interlude, which only she and her brother would share once she had met his plane; another treasured memory she could add to the thousands of others she had stored away. She explained

114

that she had to shop in town to order new school uniform. Karin, with resignation, accepted this. There was no reason, Simone thought, why she should question her movements.

As soon as she entered Marc's flat, she knew her journey was unnecessary. Looking around, she felt the trip was a futile one, and yet he seemed very close. Nothing needed attention. It was tidy, his bed made, and there was ample food in the fridge. She picked up the mail that had accumulated on the mat, placing it carefully, without bothering to sort out the junk mail, in a neat pile on his desk, before leaving the warmth of the drawing room and going into the Square.

She stood on the pavement, undecided on how to get to Knightsbridge. The Square was empty of traffic. Crossing over, she walked past the low silver railings. A slight wind played with the hydrangeas, beating their heads against dying dahlias. Tightening the scarf round her neck, she quickened her pace until she reached the main street, where she knew she would have a good chance of hailing a taxi.

Marc's stay at the chateau and his return to England had its repercussions. Simone, who had imagined a reunion fashioned to her own personal desires, found her mind sufficiently clouded by misgivings. Leo's disappointment showed in his distant attitude, his resentment stemming from fear that his brother still mistrusted him and doubted his abilities. Being the eldest child and first-born, Marc's memory of his adolescence in France was always strong and vivid, giving him a sense of conviction.

In the lounge of Leo's Harding Street flat, Marc watched them as they settled in the low, leather chairs, symmetrically arranged to form three sides of a square around a large glass-topped occasional table. His mind, taught so efficiently in the past to be observant, continued to question and examine. The symbolic regularity was something he had noticed many times before. The room was square; the carpet, the table, the ashtrays, the walls and ceiling all possessed four sides. He studied the heads of his family circle in turn. They were round, but they would later that night rest on square pillows.

Leo was tense. Karin was not present as this was during one of her regular clinic visits. He moved uncomfortably in his chair, eventually to leave it, the cushions crumpled against the arms. Marc watched his brother as he strode across the room to the piano. Leo pulled the stool from underneath it, sat down, lifted the polished lid and began tinkling the keys.

'Shouldn't we take notes?' Leo asked.

Marc put his untouched drink on the mantelpiece, his eyes searching his brother's face. Leo had a naive way of speaking, like a child.

'This isn't a board meeting,' Marc answered. 'I don't think it necessary.' He glanced at Simone. 'Does anyone else?'

'Perhaps I ought to go,' Charles moved awkwardly in his chair. 'This is family business.'

Simone's voice was full of annoyance. 'And you are a member of the family. I wasn't aware that this was a board meeting.'

'It *isn't*,' Marc repeated. 'It's a family meeting.'

'The family is the firm,' Leo categorically stated.

'Well, I'm sure Marc wants to know what's been going on,' Simone remarked.

'What do you mean?' Leo snapped. 'Nothing has been *going on*.'

Charles spoke into his almost empty glass. 'She means at the factory.'

Once again, Marc watched them. After only a few weeks away, his absence was having an effect on them but in different ways. He hoped leaving them would be beneficial, making them learn to become stronger, as they relied on him too much. However, this hope seemed to be on the brink of collapsing.

'Perhaps Simone could jot down the relevant bits?' Marc suggested.

'We do not want anything *jotted down*,' Leo said, opening a drawer in a desk and holding out a pad and ballpoint pen. 'This must be done properly.'

He passed the pad to Simone, his shaking hand causing the biro to fall to the floor. Charles bent down to retrieve it, his sudden exertion causing him to pause for breath. Only Marc appeared to notice the slight gasping and change of pallor in his brother-in-law's face.

Simone, fighting the urge not to give Marc more than a quick furtive glance, suddenly found herself scrutinising his open expression. In the subdued light, even the brightness in his eyes could not be disguised. His whole attitude unnerved her. She doodled on the pad, her actions far simpler and less of a strain than making conversation.

'Has someone got the figures?' Marc asked.

'Leo has,' Simone said, without looking up from the pad.

Leo passed Marc an unopened folder. 'It's all in there,' he said, 'right up to date.'

Marc flicked through the column of figures. He was surprised to see what had been achieved, but at the same time wondered if it had been a long enough period for Leo to accept the fact that he was completely capable. Based on what he held in his hand, he was convinced that he could turn over all authority, leaving them to manage the factory efficiently, thus leaving him free. However, that would not release the cash he required for Nuage.

Even as he thought about this, he knew he would not be free. Once he returned to Nuage, he would be beset with fresh problems, the ensuing commitments replacing those he intended handing over to Leo and Simone. It was like comparing the frying pan and the fire with the factory and the chateau. Yet, the factory was no more than a shallow dish against the cauldron of the chateau, where emotions were deep and love and hatred simmered together, never quite melting into one definite entity.

117

He suddenly spoke. 'I see you got the Comfy contract. That's very good, Leo. Very good. You're going to need that.'

Leo sat up in his chair. 'I am?' He fumbled for words. 'Why me? I don't follow your reasoning.'

Marc put the folder on the mantelpiece, took his untouched drink to a chair and sat down. He had already chosen the seat, while he surveyed them from the fireplace. It was in a strategic position, between Leo and Simone.

'I went away for two reasons. One was personal but the other concerns you all.' He paused before continuing. 'I want to sell.'

For a few seconds no one spoke. Simone had stopped doodling. To her, it seemed as if even the large clock had ceased to tick, the silence was so profound. The pause became embarrassingly long. She waited for Leo to answer. He was, she knew, quite beyond it.

'You want us to buy you out?' she asked, writing quickly.

Marc nodded. 'Naturally, you and Leo have first choice. It seems there are several courses you can follow.' He sipped at his whisky. 'You can buy me out, you can consider a merger, you can go public, or you can fold. The choice is yours.'

Leo jumped to his feet. 'Now, wait a minute!' He walked to the drinks cabinet and poured himself another. 'You know damn well the choice *isn't* solely ours. Don't pass your responsibilities on to us. What about the employees?'

Marc spoke quietly. 'It isn't a question of my responsibilities. I am handing them over to you. That is, if you want them, of course. You and Simone have first option. It has always been my intention to do this. I now feel the time has come to do it.'

'You've never spoken like this before,' Simone said. 'Why?'

'I thought you would have realised. Surely, you didn't think that I would go on forever. People do retire.'

'You! Retire?' Leo sneered. 'I don't believe it.'

118

'That is your affair,' Marc replied. 'Think about it. Obviously, it is a thing that must be carefully considered. We can discuss it in greater detail in a couple of days.'

'A couple of days!' Leo's ongoing shock was obvious.

'But what will you do?' Simone asked. 'The factory *is* you. You began it from nothing. It's your life.' Her words faded away in the stuffiness of the room. All she could think about was two rooms in a back street of the East End, with an assortment of women busily working on sewing machines. He used to take her there occasionally on Friday afternoons after meeting her from school. Those wonderful weekends, when she was allowed beyond the convent walls, had become indelibly printed on her mind. The Embankment at night, with the lights of the new Festival Hall casting reflections on the darkened waters of the Thames below. She had re-lived it many times, particularly when he repeated his movements by taking Crispin and Piers. She understood very well why her two sons enjoyed staying with Marc at his flat. Uncle Marc was fun!

'It *was* my life,' she heard him say. 'And, if I am honest, it was a life I disliked. I am going back to Nuage.'

Leo gulped his drink, automatically refilling the glass. 'So that's it. Retirement in the South of France among the olive groves.'

Marc was left unmoved by the remark. Leo had little else to offer in the way of authority, beyond cynical sarcasm.

'There won't be many olive groves once we've grubbed them out and replanted with more vines and almond trees. We have the *terroir* and I have skilled and keen workers, including one of the best *vigneurs* in the world.' Marc said.

'It's a deuce of a risk, isn't it?' Charles said, suddenly breaking his long silence.

'I wouldn't want it any other way,' Marc replied. 'It would be too easy if there were no risks attached. Life's one great gamble anyway.'

119

'Bringing out the baseness in all of us,' Simone muttered.
'Is that why you want to sell? Because there are no risks involved running a factory which produces zips?' Leo asked, his voice harsh. 'We could always go over to something more exciting. There's a lot of money in armaments. We should make a decision quickly, while we still have a factory. London isn't exactly safe.'

'I need capital,' Marc said.

Simone looked puzzled. 'You don't need to dispose of your shares. You could always get a loan with your securities and there's the holding company in the Channel Islands.'

'I'm afraid I need a great deal of money,' Marc replied, hoping his words would appease her, but knowing they would have no effect. He wished he could explain in detail how he felt. He had not always been frank with them about most of his financial transactions. It was their right to be kept well informed regarding the factory. They trusted him implicitly, or had done until now. How would they feel, he wondered, if they knew of the truth about the chateau, their father, and the Swiss bank account? Both Marc and Philippe had received some compensation from the German government. He had, as the years went by, constantly changed his will, as the money accumulated. The bulk of his estate he had always left to Piers and Crispin.

When his words finally penetrated her dazed mind, her first reaction was to feel sick. She had ceased to write, her hand clutching at the collar of Charles's jacket. Her touch was enough to make him look at her, his calm face extending an assuring smile. All she could do was turn away.

'Papa would have been proud of you,' Leo muttered, slightly drunk. 'You certainly lived up to the name.'

'Then why not live up to yours?' Marc suggested. 'Napoleon is a good enough example I would have thought.'

'You should have been christened Jesus! Then your miracles could have been performed with more authenticity.'

'If you're going to philosophise,' Marc said, 'they were both leaders.' He spoke with a brief contemptuous laugh.

'I doubt if the other had syphilis,' Leo retorted, watching Simone. Evidently, she was intrigued by the conversation. 'All clap for the Emperor!' There was a pregnant pause. 'Father did,' Leo continued, his voice gruff with contempt. 'Ask Marc, Simone. Go on, he knows!'

For the first time ever their father had been mentioned. His hazy shadow haunted Simone, filling her with a kind of terror she found impossible to explain. How was it possible to fear a man she hardly knew?

'I don't think I want to know.' She faltered, her hand slipping from Charles's collar and limply falling into his waiting hand. Her fingers felt secure, fastened by his. Whatever words Marc and Leo threw at each other, or however hard they fought verbally, it would distress her to the point of temporarily wanting to abandon all family ties.

Marc had explained only recently how important her own family was. He had illustrated it graphically, much to her displeasure at the time. But that all seemed a long time ago. Perhaps he and Leo each felt she would want to fight. If they did, she would prove them both wrong. Women only fought for what they felt was valuable and worth retaining. To her, the factory was in itself of small importance. It was Marc she wanted to keep. Without him, there was no factory. Marc Chevaud, that great example of strength, courage and shrewdness, had changed. For him it seemed pleasingly acceptable. For her it was sad and alarming.

'All this is quite irrelevant,' Marc said, getting up. 'I suggest we sleep on it. Ring me the day after tomorrow and we can finalise the whole thing.'

They all stood and prepared to leave.

'Two days!' Leo glanced at Simone. 'For God's sake! That's no time at all.'

'It is all I can spare,' Marc said, going to the door. He

121

turned, waiting for Simone to offer her lips. She remained still, her body rigid, her face pale and impassive. Immediately he guessed how she felt. He watched her as she took her coat from a chair, allowing Charles to drape it across her narrow shoulders. He was aware of the silence. He knew she would not speak for some time but she would weep. Yes, she would weep, he thought, as Charles guided her past him and into the street. She would cry just as soon as the car drove out of sight.

He turned to Leo. 'Goodnight, Leo.'

'Marc! We've got to talk.'

'Yes,' Marc replied. 'But not tonight.'

Marc thoughtfully walked to his car. All the time he kept thinking of Simone. Inside her, he knew, was an emotional volcano which would eventually erupt. He was thankful she had Charles and their two sons. The fact that she was with him was consoling and it was the one decisive factor that would help him sleep at night. That, and the vision of Nuage. Falling in love went hand in hand with a kind of instability. It could be said that he was being a little unrealistic, his objectiveness clouded by emotions and hitherto untried ideas. It did not matter any more.

14

Autumn 1948

A strange feeling overcame Marc when the light aircraft landed at Blackbushe airfield. His arrival was usually unimpeded, but he remembered previously having an open parachute above him, never in England, but usually in a distant field in France. His mind went back to when air raids were not as common, but no one relaxed, as there had been much talk of Hitler's new weapons in the shape of rockets, to be fired from hidden launching sites in France. D-Day had brought relief and consolation to a nation, but not in France, they were still occupied by impressive plans of resurrection and re-establishment.

Simone had waited over an hour for his arrival. In her haste to greet him, she dropped her handbag. It was their first meeting in several months.

'Mano, oh Mano,' she murmured. 'Thank goodness you're here.' Her anxiety stemmed from many things. As a child of the war years, she was never sure when she'd see him again; her nervousness of his flying across the Channel in bad weather; concern for his reaction to their now deteriorating elderly mother, and her own health. The menopause had brought unkind symptoms.

'Hush,' he said gently. 'I'm here now, safe and sound.'

She was grateful for his comforting words.

Charles, with the help of an elderly aunt, had rented a pleasant old cottage in the middle of the New Forest. It was safer for his mother-in-law, their own house in Winchester had too many stairs and Simone's mother had fallen more than once. Anxious for her failing health, Marc was relieved that a solution had been found.

As she drove up to the cottage gate Simone said, 'Remember your last visit? You hit your head on a beam.'

'I still have the scar,' Marc replied laughing.

She left him in darkness to draw the blinds before switching on a light.

'Is there someone with her?' he asked anxiously.

'Of course, she mustn't be left alone. It isn't safe.'

With that remark, he realised the stress Simone must be under. Remembering her warning to avoid the heavy oak beam, which was dividing the hall ceiling, he ducked his head and noticed something he had not seen on previous visits. A shudder went through him.

'Simone, why is this steel hook in the beam? Do you have any pliers?'

'It was there when we arrived.' She came through from the kitchen, drying her hands, and was horrified to witness the change in him in a few seconds.

He stood against the wall, twitching, his body movements causing his head to shake. Her first reaction was to assume he had become the victim of a seizure. She ran across to him, took his trembling left hand and gently coaxed him into the small sitting room, where a fire burned on an open hearth, its flames reflecting on the polished copper ornaments.

'Mano, tell me what is it? Are you ill?'

He could not speak. Guiding him to an armchair, she stood over his shaking body.

'Have you medication for this? How long have you had fits? Why didn't you tell me? It's all these business trips abroad; it's too much for you.'

He managed to clear his throat and spoke with mumbled words. 'It isn't a fit,' he said very slowly. 'At least not on my part. I suppose one could call it a fit of madness. *Grand mal du malfaisant,*' he muttered. 'May I have some water, please?'

'Of course,' she said and half ran back to the kitchen to fetch some. 'You won't choke will you?'

Shaking his head, he reached out to take the glass from her hand, which was also shaking. 'Dear God,' she prayed, 'not Marc, as well as mother.'

Slowly she composed herself, pulling a chair close to him. 'When you're ready,' she said, 'I want to know the whole story, every bit.'

'All right,' he sighed, passing the half-empty glass to her. 'We both need something much stronger than this.'

'I don't think so,' she replied. 'Not in your present condition. Are you hungry?'

'Not really. Café Calva would be nice, and a cigarette please.'

'Oh, all right.'

When she returned, he saw she was carrying a travelling rug. She placed it over him, concerned about his shaking body.

'Simone, I'm not cold.'

'You'll do as you're told,' she said, laughing a little. 'Now I'm just going to check *Maman*. Leo and Charles made a room for her downstairs. Leo had to return to the office, he should be back later.'

Gradually he was recovering. 'Can I see her now?' he asked.

'No,' was the affirmative reply. 'You're in no state to see her. Besides, she won't know you.'

Her final words caused him to wince.

'Are you ready for my story?'

'Yes,' she sighed. 'Marc, what is *grand mal du malfaisant*? I know the first two words relate to epilepsy. What is *malfaisant*? It's a long time since I spoke acceptable French.'

'It means *ma petite*, evil with a capital E, the very worst type of evil.' He paused. 'That is my story. A tale of evil, corruption, murder, sadism, torture, pure unadulterated wickedness. Adolf Hitler and his band of beasts have become

125

history, an episode of failure mixed with madness. I helped to work for the peace that we have now.'

'What did you do in London, during the war?' she asked.

'I worked with intelligence,' he replied, stopping to finish his cognac and coffee. She had used a lot of sugar.

Her quick mind worked rapidly and already she was several jumps ahead of him. 'But you were also in France, weren't you?'

'Yes,' he said. 'I was mostly at home in Mirabeau – what was left of the village. We were in a group of Maquisards, sabotaging and killing the Boche.'

'So, that is why Papa sent us to England.'

'Yes,' he replied. 'Shall I go on?' He sifted events in his mind, holding back the worst ones, which he knew would disturb her.

'Yes,' she said, passing him a lighted cigarette and coughing at the smoke.

'I was caught with several others and we were imprisoned by the Gestapo.' He stopped. 'We were tortured by them in Fresnes prison. They did all kinds of dreadful things to people before they executed them. Philippe Coutanche was almost starved to death in a cell of concrete, with no air and no bed. He lived on a cold, concrete floor, sitting on it, sleeping on it, eating off it, and other unspeakable things. Use your imagination. He weighed under six stone when he was released. I myself was strung from butchers' hooks by my thumbs, wetting my trousers, while the guards stood and laughed. It wasn't just me, there was a young girl next to me in a similar situation. She died after twenty-four hours and they left her, the Boche had not heard of sexual finesse, we were all filth and gangsters.'

'Did you escape?' she asked, with childish eagerness.

'No, I'm not that brave. Someone pulled strings, and guess who that was.' He looked at her, studying her face.

'I've no idea.'

'It was Papa.'

'But...' she began.

'He was on familiar terms with the Commandant at Nuage, and of course, the arms factory at Toulon.'

She shook her head. 'I don't know what you're talking about,' she whispered. 'Tell me about Nuage. Is that where I was born?'

'Yes, we all were, I'll tell you more after a good night's sleep,' he said. 'Where shall I rest my weary head?'

To her relief he had stopped trembling. She knew that it was more than being strung up on a hook, but wanted to remain ignorant about other forms of torture. Her admiration had always been great. It had now reached gigantic proportions. She kissed him and, taking his empty coffee cup, left the room to stop outside another door. Intently she listened for any sound. All she could hear was her mother's snoring. Later, in bed, she lay quiet, thinking, listening to the creaks and tapping escaping from the tired old building, releasing the numerous spirits it must contain. She closed her eyes and was asleep before she had finished saying her prayers.

Marc knew that his mother was ill. Perhaps Simone had papered over the cracks, as she had not explained how seriously their mother was deteriorating. His suspicions were proven by the fact that he had been addressed as 'Michel'. According to Simone, their mother addressed all male visitors by her husband's Christian name. His mother's condition disturbed him to a certain extent, the whole visit magnifying Simone's stress, which was obvious to him and quickly feeding his already deep depression. The whole situation brought his embedded guilt to the surface. He had recovered from physical pain, but the mental scars he possessed cut deep and fuelled his tremendous guilt. On occasions, he compared himself to the prodigal son, in the hope that his future restoration plans for Nuage at Mirabeau would placate his conscience. Perhaps results of his plans and proof of his good intentions would alleviate most of the bad memories and feelings. There was no fatted calf to be killed by a father who had destroyed a dynasty.

While with Simone at the cottage, Marc tried to establish a feeling of freedom. He took long walks in the forest where the oaks and hazels reminded him of Nuage. He had done part of his training in the South of England, freely learning how to kill the enemy. The New Forest had not changed, apart from the absence of native ponies that had once roamed freely. Simone had explained the reason. Large padlocked stockades had been erected which were guarded by verderers and a motley crew of others, including the Home Guard, who were legally entitled to carry arms. These precautions were necessary to stamp out the scourge of black marketeers, who rode the English range rounding up animals of all description. If the odd sheep got in the way, it was chased to death, saving them the problem of slaughtering it. The practice of 'lamping' was forbidden due to the regulation blackout. Rabbits, thankfully, were still plentiful.

Horseflesh was sold to unscrupulous butchers who passed it off as prime English meat. No questions asked, no coupons required. Meat was always a reliable commodity. Marc explained to his sister that the English black market was not alone. In France, it had become the norm, not stopping with meat. Much was available, nothing escaped, and the criminals responsible were easily lining their pockets, mostly from the occupying forces.

The wine pillage from the Nuage cellars suffered an identical fate, ironically enjoyed by Germans of other ranks, having gorged on questionable prime steak in the best restaurants of Paris and other reputable eating places. They lived in luxury while the majority of the French starved and died.

During his last day with Simone, Marc tried to telephone Philippe at Nuage, almost giving up after several failed attempts.

Finally, he heard Philippe's crackled voice, and Marc told him to buy a new pick-up or a small truck to replace the Renault which was ready for the scrapyard, and meet him at Marignane the following day.

15

A week later

Marc's departure from the cottage was a swift one. Tactfully, Simone had left him alone with their mother, before instructing the carer who was relatively new to the Comtesse. In a few minutes, Marc placed a small leather jewellery box on her chest, which barely moved with her shallow breathing. Gently he lifted her right hand, placing it on the medal he had been awarded, then he put the empty box on a side table, kissed her tenderly and hurriedly left the room. He was ready for Simone to drive him to catch his plane, hoping that Philippe would be there to meet him.

Philippe knew exactly how and where to get a vehicle: in a back street of Paris hidden in a suburb, close to the Fontenay-en-Laye. Before the war, a large and busy auto outlet sold second-hand vehicles, most of them stolen. Like most other business concerns, the occupying forces had completely taken it over during the war, using the depot as a channel for replacements of their own transport.

Philippe's informant, a former Resistance friend, had given him details of a cache of new Renaults and commercial vehicles in good working order. The Resistance had become experts at stealing, an act that was not without danger, as heavy street fighting had been rife and shooting indiscriminate. Stealing a vehicle had been relatively simple, obtaining petrol was not so easy.

'You see!' Philippe boomed, 'Would you like the key?'

'That would be useful,' laughed Marc.

'We have the very latest design, thanks to Boche ingenuity. You just push a button; let me show you.'

'No, you drive,' Marc said. 'I'm tired of all the button-pushing that's required of me these days.'

'What about women?' Philippe remarked.

Marc ignored this. 'I'm starving,' he said, 'for food and news. And I haven't got the strength, or inclination for anything else.'

Simone's telephone call was not expected. Her calls were frequent with family news, but she had already spoken to him earlier that day. Her distressing message was given to him in short bursts, the words hesitant, though not totally choked. Then she gave way and every sentence was broken by suppressed sobs, followed by intermittent bouts of weeping.

Accepting the news of his mother's death, he felt both instant grief and tremendous relief. During quiet reflective periods back in France at Nuage, he had felt his mother was brought closer to him. Maybe I'm growing senile or paranoid, he thought. There were times when he could almost feel her presence. On one occasion, he could swear he smelt her perfume.

Fate had been unkind to la Comtesse. Married young, the early years of marriage to his father had been, perhaps, perfect. Recently this once beautiful, sophisticated, chic lady, who had possessed everything, was no longer treated with the respect she had received in the past. He thought of her constantly, but the pleasant memories were not quite strong enough to erase the awful truth of hypocritical non-progress, which Simone repeated. Their darling mother, no longer a figure of poise, charm and a quick intelligent brain, had lost her dignity. She had reverted to the behaviour and posture of an infant being fed in a high chair.

'Imagine her strapped into a hard wooden chair,' Simone had said. It was unbearable to witness scenes like that. The tray in front of her holding a bowl of sloppy food, with medication crushed into it, making it easier for her to swallow tablets. She wet herself unknowingly and stared into space to talk to demons. Thoughts of her incontinence jerked Marc back to his own past, but his own lack of bladder control had been induced by pain from incessant beating and vicious kicking in the region of his damaged organs. There was a paradox – la Comtesse had lost her dignity; with difficulty, he managed to retain his own.

He was grateful to Simone and Leo, both had been most supportive. The kindness of others made him aware of his own feelings of guilt which were suffocating him. He heard Simone's voice, which sounded more composed now.

'Mano, are you still there?'

'Yes,' he eventually replied, 'still here.'

'Can we get her to France?'

'No, there are regulations, it would be very difficult.'

'Can't we have her buried with Papa in the family vault?'

'Oh God,' he thought. He had to tell her, but this was not the right time. Besides their father's disappearance, the vault no longer existed.

'Mano, speak to me.'

He cleared his throat. 'Simone, I don't know where Papa is.' There was a lump in his throat.

'What are you trying to tell me? Do you have to be so evasive?'

'Papa isn't buried anywhere.'

'What!' she exclaimed in dismay.

'There was nothing to bury. Go to the French Embassy in London and take Charles for moral support.'

Bursting into a fresh flood of tears, she replaced the receiver. Crispin stood by her side and searched for her hand. Taking it into his own stained, sticky fingers, he squeezed.

'Papa should be home soon,' she said, 'tell me when you hear the car door slam. Have you finished making your model aeroplane?' Dutifully he left her, sensing she wanted solitude. She was still crying when Charles unlocked the front door, dropped his briefcase to the floor and took his grief-stricken wife in his arms.

16

Mirabeau 1968

Hans Grich stood beneath the awning of the Bar des Pêcheurs, watching the slowly moving traffic that crept behind the village square. Behind him, the large window was smothered by condensation. He knew he had to stay in the background and not become involved in any local disputes. It was almost a scene of déjà vu. Mirabeau-en-ciel was imprinted on his mind; he had been there after the war as a tourist.

Customers were now leaving the bar, noisy groups of men arguing as they left the smoke-filled rooms. They passed him without a second look and continued to walk with drunken steps until out of sight.

He waited for a few moments before leaving. Going in the opposite direction, he felt disappointed that he had not observed Marc Chevaud – it was not so urgent, but he had need of information.

The rain had eased. Hans walked quickly with his head raised, slowing down to allow a group of men to pass him. It was the future now, time for him to create his own life with Rudi, his sister's fatherless son, whom he had unofficially fostered. He had been pleased to have an intelligent pupil, but the stupid boy had made the fatal mistake of lusting after the bailiff's granddaughter, Marie-Jeanne. Sadly, his decision to send his nephew home to Germany was a final one; the last thing he wanted was a French bastard baby to arrive to complicate already troublesome matters.

Later, both Hans and Marc lay in a certain amount of discomfort. Grich, on a folding bed, attempted to stretch his legs in the temporary accommodation of his camper van.

Marc had no need to tell Philippe how tired he felt. The morning came later than usual but he was disturbed by noises of machinery. The crashing of a jackhammer resounded across heaps of stones and the grinding of a crane's caterpillar tracks grated against stone, as walls tumbled to the ground. There was also the constant whine of a circular saw as it cut through well-seasoned wood.

His reaction was to bury his head beneath a crumpled pillow, surrendering to what seemed to be an insurmountable problem. In exasperation, he got up and pushed at a window. Had he known, no force was needed to free the rotten frame and a pane of glass dropped to the bare floor, shattering with a loud crash.

There was no pain, only a pool of blood spreading across his bare foot. Swearing, he retreated, his efforts to avoid fragments of jagged glass not easy. One foot was an inconvenience, he needed two that both worked. Attempting to staunch the flow of blood, he hopped to the ancient sink, gasping as the coldness of fresh water touched the open wound, colouring the water pink.

In twisting and lifting his foot from the sink, he lost his balance and found himself suddenly being held by Philippe.

'We must not be seen like this,' Marc remarked, smiling. 'Would it not be a compromising position?' The shaggy eyebrows above clear brown eyes appeared to smile. Relaxed, the brows no longer met. 'It's a bloody awkward position and I'm getting cramp.'

'Perhaps I should help you back to your damaged bed,' Philippe suggested.

'That would be a more disreputable situation,' Marc replied, grabbing his bailiff's shoulder, his action causing his face to be closer than before. Unlike his own cheek, he felt stubble against his.

After a few seconds passed, he said, 'I never knew you cared.'

'*Bien sur*. You need a doctor, for sure. You will require stitching. Dr Barrault will be delighted to stop your blue blood from escaping.'

'Dr who?'

'Barrault. His blood is red, very red, I assure you. He's a commy.'

'What happened to Dr Blum?' Marc enquired of their family doctor, who had been a pillar of respect and had carefully delivered Simone.

Philippe shrugged his shoulders, loosening Marc's hand. With Gallic indecisiveness, he shrugged and waved his hands. 'Who knows, who cares? He was marched off to a concentration camp with other Israelites. I believe they shot him.'

'You'd better take me now,' Marc said, with resignation. 'I may bleed to death.'

'*Domage*,' Philippe murmured.

In the late dawn the next day, small slivers of light pushed their way through ancient, blemished shutters. Although the bed was acceptably comfortable, despite its inadequate length, Marc's exhaustion was too much to care about comfort and, wide-awake, a thousand memories and ideas flooded his fatigued mind. Lying there he studied the ceiling just above him, the many cracks now zigzagged into a bizarre pattern, causing him to remember the razor-wire on the stone grey walls of his prisons. Fresnes, the hated place of detention: to be incarcerated in such a godforsaken place meant to be doomed to extinction unless a miracle occurred. He had no time for such beliefs; even an after-life had become questionable. The evidence of cruelty, the destruction of materialism and reasonable ideology, was replaced by sadism and the belief in insane diatribes from a despotic maniac who followed the dictate of his personal astrologer and who was an addict to valerian.

His stitched foot was telling him he should move it to stop the pins and needles sensation. Think of pleasant things, he told himself. It is all in the past. Fresnes, Mont Valérian and Cherche-Midi, those dreadful, unspeakable places, all belonged to yesterday. One place led to another, and finally to the woods at Nuage, with Sylvie's untimely death from terrible torture.

Sometimes his thoughts were acceptable, remembering her sweet smile. He had a favourite memory, the long leisurely walks they used to share on visits to Sault and the lavender fields. 'Flowers dance in Provence': how well he remembered the poem learnt at school.

> *In Provence*
> *flowers dance!*
> *A floral ballet*
> *Chasséz!*
> *Pas de deux*
> *of bleu.*
> *Chorus line of bending stalks*
> *Audience of tourists*
> *As it stands*
> *then slowly walks*
> *on beaten paths*
> *Across blue lands.*
>
> *The stage is set –*
> *Backdrop of hills,*
> *Green, purple, brown,*
> *falling down*
> *Flat-roofed houses of white*
> *Clinging to stone,*
> *Throwing shadows*

Barrier against the heat,
Puffed up clouds drifting
Across squares of golden corn
Acres of ripening wheat meet
A haze of blue.

Burnished gold
The corn is like your hair
Strong, shining
No buttercup here felt frost,
Yellow sleeping heads unfold
wearing bonnets,
Poppies dressed in red
Living in this Eden,
Paradise of wondrous hours
Never to be lost,
Timed by the whispering of a million
perfumed flowers.

Sylvie never grew tired of listening to him as he recited the words, implanted in his brain by a strict M'selle, who unfortunately for her was of Jewish extraction, and was ultimately led away with hundreds of others, never to be seen again.

17

Whistling for his dog, Philippe walked in the direction of the lane leading to Germaine's crêperie. Undaunted by the queue waiting to give their orders, he tied the dog's lead to a chair leg outside, and patiently waited for the queue to shrink. Philippe caught her alert eye, and Germaine waved, beckoning him to draw closer.

'I'm all out!' she complained. 'Do you think Marie-Jeanne could come and give me a hand? An extra pair of hands and feet would be useful.'

'Call her on the telephone,' he said. 'Tell her I said she must come right away.'

'Bless you,' she said, and went back to wiping her counter.

Marie-Jeanne had not completely recovered from Rudi's sudden and unexplained departure.

During the war the Boche had put a stop to any hope of a woman forming a relationship with a French male, as these were transported to unknown places, forced into slave labour or held captive in camps. Some were conscripted into the German army. In the case of Vichy France, they were to serve in the Milice.

After the war there was a mere handful of men left in Mirabeau. Those that returned in a disorderly fashion were mostly broken men, many still in their youth, which they had lost to look like old men. The sick, the old, and those like Marc and Philippe, they bore the scars of beatings, whippings and evidence of general deprivation.

Marie-Jeanne accepted that she would have to stay and perhaps spend the rest of her life in a commune that lived and died for the production of wine. Her ambition was to leave and join the outside world. She had read about it in books. The idea of running away had occurred to her, but it was a non-starter. She had no money to call her own.

The offer of work at the crêperie was too good to refuse and the wages would be useful. There would be tips from the tourists too. They were beginning to arrive in coach-loads from everywhere, consisting mainly of Americans and Germans. The latter wanted to visit the makeshift graves where bodies had been namelessly buried. On the day of the great exodus in 1944, dead casualties were left in piles, littering the once grand frontage of Chateau Nuage. Bodies floated in the ornate pond where koi had once played and happily blown bubbles. The fish had long disappeared, eaten by starving soldiers who mashed the flesh into tins of cold sauerkraut and devoured the contents with relish.

Philippe put some coins on the counter. 'Watch her, please,' he said.

'I'll be a mother to her,' Germaine said, pocketing the money. 'She will not be overworked, I promise.'

Philippe and the dog took their time returning to the cottage. Now, without Marie-Jeanne, everything was changing he thought, unleashing the dog, which immediately lay by his chair waiting for his master to sit.

Hans knew from the moment he threw the duvet off his uncomfortable bed that he had to discuss his decision with someone in charge at the chateau. It had to be today and not postponed until tomorrow.

Snatching a stale croissant from the kitchen table, he called the two dogs, whose tails brushed the closed door with eager monotony, their eyes fixed lovingly on their master. He clipped on their leads to pull at the leather straps of his ex-army binoculars and his Leica camera. The dogs made no movement, waiting for words of command. As soon as he spoke the words they had learned to respect and dutifully respond to, they leapt from the camper van, pulling the leads from his hands and raced to the closed temporary gate, where they waited for the next command. Their daily exercise followed a regular routine. To be free from the confines of the van was a joyous occasion for both animals and master.

All of them shared the fresh air, taking time to absorb breathtaking views, where virgin mornings and an advancing sun would snatch every opportunity to capture shadows of deep purple and the sweet, pungent perfume of wild native flora.

Hans turned across an open field, heading towards the stone boundary walls of Nuage and his own much smaller property.

Stopping to hoist the various leather straps which annoyingly kept slipping from his shoulder, he called the dogs, who were excitedly jumping up against the stones of a half-collapsed wall. Their frantic barking was possibly because of a terrified rabbit, crouching and trembling behind the wall.

Early morning! The best time of day. He had become tired with his constant spying on Marc and all the hectic activities at the chateau. It seemed it had become an obsession. The very first memory he had of Mirabeau was when he arrived as a guide to conduct a tour of fellow Germans. Once more, his faithful camera and field glasses accompanied him whenever he felt his wanderings were inescapable. The acreage he bought with the abandoned manor was not big enough for him.

Boundary stone walls tend to collapse. Here in beautiful Provence it was often due to wild boars burrowing and routing into the soil, disturbing foundations weak and dilapidated from neglect. Something would be done about the *sangliers*, once his planned business venture had become an ongoing and profitable scheme. He would have the walls and old fences repaired.

Calling the dogs back he knew he would need help from Marc Chevaud, or a person like him, someone who had been born in the region, a man who others regarded as an up-to-date landlord, steeped in the ancient, almost feudal laws, governing life in a small French rural place. Possession through inheritance. Mirabeau and Nuage were not a debatable territory. Almost everyone in the area looked up to the man who lived and owned the castle, not in civility, but with deep respect and unhidden feelings of loyalty. Ever since the war, a simmering anger existed. Hans needed workers to rebuild and restore his own derelict house, possibly as old as the chateau if not older. Long ago, he concluded that he and the omnipresent patron had things in common. Marc was omnipresent.

Numerous times when he took the dogs and the new rifle out hunting, he found himself trespassing, walking on the vast Chevaud estate, where *cerf* grazed safely in dignified silence. The area was teeming with game – rabbits, pigeon and boar were plentiful here, thankfully gradually returning to their natural habitat to live in safety, now that the enemy had fled. Occasionally he shot and killed an ibex for the sheer pleasure it gave him, to kill a strong wild mountain goat that had wandered from its rocky precipitous shelter to enjoy fresh pasture. There was no gain in the killing; ibex meat was tough with a very strong flavour. During wartime, it would have been acceptable at an empty table, for hungry people waiting with empty stomachs. An ibex hunt was not the type he enjoyed. Hans had a different idea of game to play. He needed information on an unsolved mystery, a puzzle that had been nagging at him for several years.

A rising dawn with its habitual promise of warmth and light greeted the army of labourers, all unshaven and dressed in the ubiquitous workers' 'blues'. Work had already begun by six a.m. Hans surmised that it was going to be a mammoth task before the restoration was completed. A huge amount of money in cash for the Chevauds was not a problem. His own father had told him of the priceless paintings at the chateau, with Van Gogh and Gauguin much in evidence. He was envious of his father, who had known the place before the ravages of war which had wrought unbelievable and unnecessary destruction of wanton violation, defacing a national monument of outstanding splendour. No matter how much time or money it cost, Marc was prepared to spend as much as he could obtain on the restoration. This once beautiful edifice, a happy family home over centuries, could never again become the outstanding residence it had once been. The Comte's workers were very skilled, and probably descendants of the original artisans who had been involved in the beginning of founding and creating of this example of exquisite perfection.

A meeting with M'sieur le Comte had to be arranged that day, if possible. Hans walked back in the direction of his property, which like the chateau had half a roof and many other defects. Within its broken walls a tree was growing, in the centre of what had once been a large room.

Since returning Rudi to his mother, he admitted to himself how much he missed the young man. Not simply his companionship, but all the useful tasks he performed. He had proved to be a passable chef, a pastime for which Hans had no flair or inclination. Thoughts of food made him aware he had not eaten for several hours. Suddenly he stopped dead in the wooded lane; the aroma of coffee and other gastronomic goodies filled the still morning air. Temptation stirred, not only in the cafetière but also in caramelised cherry syrup, sweet to his nose, all very tempting to those in proximity of the counter.

Germaine carried on grinding beans, in no hurry to be civil or polite as he pulled out a plastic chair to sit at an empty table. Then she saw the two dogs, their noses to the tiled floor, sniffing and licking the well-trodden tiles with investigative curling pink tongues, cleaning the floor of grains of sugar and recently spilt jam.

Annoyed, she stopped the grinder. 'M'sieur, no dogs in here, they must remain outside.'

He stared at her with soulless eyes, his face expressing no answer to her words. His mind returned to an incident in a fashionable Paris restaurant during the occupation. At the time he was waiting to be served. He watched a well-dressed woman at an adjacent table and noticed a waiter walking towards her, leading a snow-white standard poodle, perfectly groomed. The dog, as chic as his mistress, was lifted onto a chair opposite its owner. A bib was then placed around the animal's neck. Hans had become used to the French idiosyncrasies that were Paris a long time ago. Few changes had been made. Small hope for the poodle, as dogs became scarce in a city of hungry people.

'Of course, madame, I will tie them to a table leg.'

'Not in here,' she said curtly. 'There are metal rings outside in the wall.' As an afterthought she asked, 'Will you take coffee?'

'Please,' he replied. 'And are there any pastry cakes?'

'I have only crêpes left.'

He ordered a plate of two and devoured them, as a starving man would eat. She watched him through half-closed eyes. He was just like the rest of them; they lacked manners too. After he had finished his fourth crêpe and third cup of coffee, he watched her as she cleaned the tables, wiping them with a damp cloth.

Both were playing games, the cat wanting to pounce on the mouse, taking their time, to each other's annoyance. She wanted to close for the day and he knew it.

At last he spoke. 'Madame, the bill please, I have not paid.'

'Zut!' She swore under her breath, she had forgotten the bill and swiftly produced it from her overall pocket.

Opening his wallet, he withdrew some notes and a small

wad of photos dropped on to the table she had earlier cleaned. Picking up a loose one, she clearly saw the face of someone from the past. Her heart missed a beat – she had known the man in the picture. Her eyes stared in horror at the German officer, in the dreaded black uniform they all hated so much. Gunther Frie looked back at her. The hard, cold, dispassionate face turned her blood cold, even from a photograph.

Hans held out his hand for the return of it. Her own was trembling. Why was this man, now sitting in her café, carrying a photo of a despised SS officer – why? Both of them remained silent, but he knew she had seen something, enough. He wished to hide. In no hurried fashion, he left the premises, unleashing the dogs. On the way home, he took a longer route, to pass the chateau and stop to have a talk with Marc Chevaud.

18

Flinging on a coat, Germaine left for Nuage, as it was there she knew she would find Philippe. He was always there, being the conscientious bailiff he was. She found him in the devastated, once beautiful, garden at the front of the chateau, surrounded by huge mysterious piles of objects, recently delivered, and covered by black plastic sheeting and tarpaulins. She called him, and he looked up from inspecting a wooden case.

Waving, he waited for her to join him.

'What on earth's all this?' she asked.

'Stand back,' he replied, 'and I'll show you.' He pulled a cover from the nearest stack. 'They may bite!'

'Lavatories!' she exclaimed. 'And what will happen to them?' How ridiculous, she thought. The former grand spectacle, now half in ruins, sleeping in the fading sun – it was a scene of sadness and solitude. 'Toilets – there must be hundreds here!' she exclaimed.

'Not exactly,' he said, replacing the protective sheeting. 'Seventy-five, plus matching basins, some bidets and a dozen baths. Part of the deal Marc's had to consent to for the official funding with the restoration, is to open the chateau and winery to the public, so these are mostly toilets for the visitors. Did you want something? As you can see, I am otherwise engaged.'

'At least you won't have to find a hedge when nature calls,' she said. 'I have to talk to you now, it is most urgent.'

The tone of her voice was evidence of how serious she was.

'OK,' he sighed. 'I must sit down, my back's killing me.'

They sat on a flat piece of coping and shared a cigarette. He was a good listener and as she spoke he noted her voice change in tone, from a soft whisper to an angry outburst of invective.

She ended her diatribe. 'If I could, I'd kill him!'

'No, you would not.' he replied. 'Think woman, what good would it do if you did? I used to think like that when Frie was alive.' He spoke softly, shifting his gaze to his gloved fingers.

'What makes you think he's dead?' she asked.

'Just a gut feeling,' he lied. 'I bet my life if this could be proved.' Instinctively he knew he had to tell her the truth, a revelation was imminent. Slowly, he stood, stretched his aching back and began to walk away.

'Philippe,' she called, 'where are you going?'

'To find the truth.' He stopped, turned and beckoned. 'I have to sort out the plumber. Go home, Germaine, and put on some coffee. I'll meet you there in half an hour.' Carefully he stepped over loose planks of wood lying across the path.

His dismissal was final. When the Comte was in England, Philippe appeared to have been adopted as the head man to whom the people went in confidence for advice. A strong feeling of relief swept over her and for the first time in many years she was overcome by a sense of peace of mind. In his usual manner, Philippe had hardly spoken as she had related the exposure of Hans Grich's existence. Philippe was her rock and possibly her passport to freedom.

He had left Nuage before she had reached her cottage. Unlike her, his footsteps were hurried and he arrived at the cottage a few minutes before her. They talked until the early hours of the morning. He talked while she listened. The constant cups of coffee enabled them both to remain awake. His relating of his killing Gunther Frie only came as a half-surprise to her. His reticence on the subject was not abnormal. Philippe had always been a man of few words: those he managed to utter were always meaningful and guarded. On

147

many occasions the question of his coping with Gestapo interrogations reappeared, and just how much he hid during those dreadful inquisitions, knowing his torture would probably be ultra-severe.

'May I have a cognac?' he eventually asked.

'Of course.' She went to the bottles displayed on a shelf behind him, carefully choosing the very best brandy she could find. As he drank, her eyes never left him.

'What are you going to do now? You will have to tell the Seigneur? The builders will find the evidence.'

'Certainly, I will have to tell M'sieur Marc. As for the builders or anyone else, nothing will be found.'

'Yes, but what...'

He drained his glass, 'I'll think of something,' he answered quietly. Holding out his glass, she took it and refilled it. Perhaps, she thought, too much drink will loosen his tongue.

'You and I will dispose of any evidence. Finish the brandy, the whole bottle if you wish. We'll leave as soon as it's light.' She pushed her glass away.

'We will?' he said bewildered.

'But now we shall sleep.'

'I'll sleep in my own bed,' he said quietly.

'As you wish.' She went to the door, allowing a pleasant draught to enter the room. 'Goodnight Philippe.'

'Goodnight,' he mumbled and left her wondering.

Surprisingly, Philippe surrendered to sleep with his dog beside his aching body. His final thoughts of the day were of a sombre nature. Maybe I should retire, he thought, I am too old for all this.

He spoke to the dog. 'Do you agree? We've had an interesting life you and me. Are you ready to be put to pasture?' he asked, patting the dog's head as he closed his eyes, shutting out the shadows of the night. The last sounds he heard were contented grunts from the shaggy ball of fur lying with acceptable pleasure across his feet.

*   *   *

Philippe set his intentions before he fell into a deep sleep. He decided to tell Marc the news Germaine had given him and to confess his killing of Frie.

However, Marc had his own plans. The next day they drove to Arles, their conversation mostly concerning the vineyards and pay rises for the employees. The road snaked and Marc's driving was fast, his foot still paining him, while Philippe gripped a black leather case containing a large amount of cash they had withdrawn from the bank.

'I think they should be like me – I have to have a monthly cheque, why do you pay the others in cash?'

'Because that is my choice. If you prefer cash, you only have to say. That stocking in your hearth with all your savings must be pretty full by now. Pull over at the next bar-tabac. I need a peepee stop and tobacco.'

His need to talk was acute. While sitting in silence he rehearsed what he wished to say to his employer, who appeared to be tense and short-tempered. Perhaps he should postpone his planned confession.

It was simple to relieve the pressure on his full bladder, but more difficult to stem the flow of thoughts in his much-occupied mind. They drank wine and smoked for a while until Marc asked, 'What's on your mind, Philippe?'

'Plenty,' he answered into his glass. 'I want to tell you something which has been on my mind for some time,' he finally said.

'Not on your conscience?' Marc asked. 'Come on, let's have it. I'm no priest!'

Philippe smoked thoughtfully. 'Most certainly not.'

'And I'm no saint,' came Marc's reply. 'I want to inspect the cellars before that pompous little prick from Paris gets his long nose into them.'

'All of them?' Philippe asked, a slight tremor in his voice.

149

'Yes, all sixty.' Marc replied.

Philippe's heart missed a few beats. He had no choice but to go along with Marc's plans.

'There won't be any wine left; the Boche took almost everything before they left.'

'Do you still have a duplicate key?' Marc asked him.

'Yes, it never left me. Your father entrusted me with it and asked me to guard it well.'

'Good.' Marc said, standing. 'Let's get back as soon as possible. I'm not entirely comfortable with all this ready cash we're carrying.'

Another pretentious young official assessor was in the inner courtyard and he walked towards them as they approached the stone steps. 'It is advisable,' he announced, 'that no one goes down below!' He was shouting above the noise of the bulldozer. 'Your *caves* are out of bounds as the north wall is unstable.'

Marc, incensed by the arrogance of this fussy individual, replied, 'Look, this is my property, and I'll damn well go where I wish.' He began to walk away.

'It is too dangerous, the structure above is unstable. It is on your head.'

'That's what my great-grandfather said,' Marc stated acidly, 'when he was herded to the guillotine. They tried to blow this place up during the Revolution, but they failed.'

Philippe listened, amused by their banter and thought it provident if the place did collapse. Frie's body still had to be there, and a pile of covering rubble would be a suitable grave.

Philippe had not been down to the cellars of the chateau for some time. Marc had thoughtfully slipped a torch into his pocket.

'There's nothing to see,' Philippe said. 'They took practically everything.'

'From the umpteenth time you've said that, I'm beginning to think you're hiding something from me. It was at the end of June 1944. Do you remember those days? Of course, I wasn't here. After D-Day I'd been sent to Paris, where the action was. Jacques Petit was with me and Sebastian Friocourt became official interpreter in the German section. We were there throughout that mess.'

'There was mess here too!' Philippe remarked. 'A bloody confused mess. The troops just panicked and there was absolute chaos. Hundreds of them were running all ways, knocking things over, carrying pictures, furniture, rugs and crates of wine. Some of the wine was in casks so they had to roll them.' He had to take a break and catch his breath. 'I was standing by the west wall, what could I do? I thought I could hide down here in case they took me hostage.'

'Where was the officer in charge when all this was happening? In Paris, we were shooting looters. Where was Frie?'

'Frie was supposed to be giving orders, but he was running with the rest. Then I found him, hiding, waiting for me at the bottom of the steps, with a Corporal who had an axe. He demanded the key from me, put his Walther pistol to my head and laughed. I did as I was told and he told the Corporal to leave.'

The fireproof door was ajar and an obnoxious smell choked them. Marc held a handkerchief to his nose as the smell caused him to gag. 'Someone's been here before us!' Marc exclaimed. 'This place stinks of death. You and I are well baptised in the stench of death.'

'Let's get out of here,' Philippe said, 'I can't breathe.'

'No,' Marc replied. 'Look at this place.' The cement floor was littered with broken glass, smashed bottles, wine stains, and other dark stains that Marc knew were dried blood.

Oak casks lay broken in a haphazard fashion. Marc saw it first. It lay on a bed of glass fragments.

'What in the hell happened here?' He finally asked, of no one in particular.

Philippe stared at the grotesque sight. With an expression of disbelief, he shook his head.

'Dear God, no one has been here to my knowledge since I killed him.'

Marc flashed the torch across the remains of Gunther Frie. 'Are you quite sure you did?'

'Absolutely. It has to be him, look at the uniform.'

'What's left of it,' Marc said.

They gazed at the skeleton, still dressed in the hated SS uniform, now in tatters, ripped in places by unknown predators.

'What's the answer?' Marc asked.

'There is only one,' Philippe concluded. 'Rats! This place was always infested with them. I was forever telling your father.' He kicked at the once pristine black leather boots absent of heels, which had been gnawed away.

'Let's go,' Marc said. 'Find Remy. Tell him to bring a wheelbarrow and we'll take this bag of bones to another resting place.'

'My honest opinion is to burn it.'

'He's already there, Philippe, down in the ovens of hell.' Marc spoke no more. Philippe had already left, grateful to breathe fresh air.

19

Ever since the dreadful revelation in the cellars, Philippe had not left Marc's side. There were still questions that needed answering. Marc knew that Philippe would tell him the whole story, not through feelings of guilt, but through huge relief.

Later they sat on the tailboard of a lorry, staring into the warm, sultry evening. Marc broke the silence. 'I still don't understand, you hit Gunther Frie over the head with a bottle of my father's wine?'

'Yes,' said Philippe. 'It was a grand cru.' His words were sorrowful.

Marc burst out laughing, with Philippe sharing his amusement.

'Yes,' Philippe said in a mournful tone, 'I believe it was a 1929.'

Their shared laughter echoed through the stillness of the evening, into the mountains and along the valleys.

'Tell me the rest,' Marc gently coaxed.

'Well,' Philippe began. 'You know that a good *vigneron* always carries vine ties in his pocket and as a good Maquisard, I had been well taught the art of garrotting quickly and easily.'

Marc smiled. 'And...' he coaxed.

'A pity he did not feel much, the clout with the bottle only knocked him out for a bit. I wanted him to suffer as so many of us did. I wanted him to beg me to stop.'

'It's all yesterday, water under the bridge, Philippe.'

'Not my bridge,' Philippe said wistfully. 'The Boche blew it up like the rest.'

Bored and anxious to proceed with his plans, instead of returning home, Hans walked with slow determined steps, searching for Marc. The soft blue light of a magical dusk settled on the surroundings, almost blotting out the spectacle of the hideous building site. He had no need to see this scene clearly, he could hear men's voices, loud and angry sounds of shouting, mixed with vociferous proof that tempers had risen to abusive language, verging on physical violence, threats. He smiled. Perhaps another problem for the Anglo-French gentleman.

Marc had frequently argued with the Ministry of Ancient Buildings and Monuments and was questioning his decision: was he doing the right thing? He blamed himself for not thinking it out and not fully realising what red tape would be involved. The bureaucracy concerning the restoration of Nuage was the epitome of French officialdom. Curtly he wished the men in their smart suits goodnight. He heard dogs barking somewhere, close by.

Hans stopped walking, killing a few moments of time. 'I see you are very busy,' he remarked. 'I do not wish to disturb you and your visitors.'

'That is no problem,' Marc said. 'They're just men from the Ministry, nosy civil servants.'

Impatiently Hans's dogs began to pull at their leads. He quietly ordered them to stop. 'And which ministry is that?' he asked.

'The one that deals with old buildings of historical interest.'

'And yours is?' Hans questioned. The stab of sarcasm was apparent.

'Of course. It was originally built a hundred years before the Revolution. It was in 1789 when the rabble tried to pull it down and dragged my ancestors away to visit Madame la Guillotine.'

'How very remiss of them.' Hans, tired of the French saga, kicked a loose stone with a foot. 'How many labourers do you have? I myself need help with my property. I can pay them well.' The last words were meant as a jibe.

Marc had often wondered how the German had acquired his obvious wealth. 'I am sure you would if the situation arose. We have a long way to go yet. You should speak to my bailiff, Philippe Coutanche. He keeps a sharp eye on things.'

Marc's words were exactly what Hans wanted to hear. It was Philippe he wanted to see. Coutanche was regarded as a local hero, a man of the soil, a person who had been a long and faithful servant to both the lord and the domain of Mirabeau. It was a known fact that he was a Resistance hero.

Marc knew Hans was loathed by all. Maybe he would finish what the red hats of the Revolution had failed to do, destroy all that encompassed Nuage and its environmental assets.

Hans's train of thought was brought to a halt when Marc spoke again.

'He'll be somewhere inside the house, probably at the rear of the inner courtyard.'

'Thank you,' Hans said courteously.

Hans found the men he wanted to see, and hung back out of sight, watching, as they stood by a stationary tractor, deep in conversation. To his surprise, Germaine was with them. She remained silent and motionless. They stopped their conversation and greeted Marc, unusually in a manner Hans thought indifferent. Quickly he gave them orders and waited for their reaction. It was strange, as Hans had expected questions. Marc repeated his urgent plea and they turned to Germaine.

'Have you found a barrow?' Remy asked her.

'No, not Germaine, this is no place or job for a lady,' said Philippe.

She laughed. 'Lady! Why, that's the best compliment I've

155

had in years, I expect the job we're doing is a removal one and I've done that before, as you know, Philippe.'

'All right, bring the barrow round to the steps in the inner courtyard.'

She mockingly saluted him and trundled off with her charge. The once corpulent body of Gunther Frie, now reduced to skeletal form, was not heavy, but difficult to move. Parts of him kept falling off and were left lying on the ground. Hans could hear them whispering, intermingled with Philippe's wheezing and Benoit's heavy breathing.

Annoyed, Philippe noticed it had taken them almost an hour to load the barrow, after a long discussion over who would push it to the smaller lake. This in itself was not going to be easy, through a wood of tangled roots and bomb craters. Philippe also reminded them that there were perhaps still some unexploded bombs or undetected mines.

Unknown to them, the silent onlooker, Hans Grich, watched every step the figures took. They tripped across the inhospitable ground, with the macabre sight of an arm hanging over the side of the barrow, still clothed in a tattered black sleeve, visible with Hans's powerful ex-army field glasses. Hans had seen all that he needed, he decided, squatting on his haunches by the two dogs. He knew! At last, he knew. Gut instinct was usually infallible. He saw the object being slipped into the deep water with hardly any disturbance of the surface. Thick, tangled, black weed beds and the unseen watcher bore witness to their actions.

Hans eventually found him, where Marc had suggested, back in the inner courtyard, tinkering with a tractor. There was no question in Hans's mind as to what he was going to do. He walked quickly, his steps silent and unheard by Philippe, who continued to bend over the bonnet of the vehicle, totally unaware of Hans standing behind him. Seizing a starting handle, which lay on the driving seat, Grich raised it, bringing it down on Philippe's head. Then he paused. What was the use of killing an old man who probably only had a short time to live anyway? He dropped the handle, which fell with a thud on a pile of sand. A silent feeling of disgust swept over him and he walked away, remembering the dogs, who had disappeared into the gloom to chase a rabbit. They were more important than an accident to a former peasant.

Reaching the edge of the wood he heard excited barking. Hunting dogs were natural swimmers, expert at retrieving game from shallow or deep water. His were no exception and their barking grew more vociferous as each moment passed. Hans was anxious to find them, to discover what their problem was. The sounds of splashing water guided him to the lake. He called the animals, but his calls were wasted, their excitement too great. Despondency mixed with anger, he began to walk away, assuming they would eventually follow him. Suddenly he turned his ankle in a hidden hole, stumbled and cursed aloud.

Impatiently he called them again and, out of nowhere, two bedraggled hounds appeared, ran to him and sat obediently at his feet. One held an object in its clenched jaw. It had brought his master a present. He loosened the lace on his boot; it was not a good moment to sprain an ankle.

The dog stared up at him in eagerness. Hans bent over to take the bony shape from the animal's mouth and the hound's grip tightened. Coaxing it, he felt the dog's jaw relax and slowly he prised a skull from between its teeth.

'Hello, Father.'

20

Germaine left Philippe in a rough temporary wooden shed, which housed tools and bags of cement, while she went to get help. Suddenly, Philippe was seized with a surge of angry confusion. The pain in his head seemed to crush his eyes and everything began to sway.

He struggled to his feet and with Remy's help staggered back into the yard. The excavator began to move towards him, yet he could hear no engine. Jumping clear, he tripped and fell to the ground. He knew he had to attack the driver, before he himself was knocked down and crushed to death. His confusion became worse. It was the imaginary driver or him. His head was throbbing violently, his shirt soaked in blood and sweat. The parked vehicle was waiting for him to drive away. The wave of madness left him and, climbing aboard the excavator, he found temporary sanity. Fumbling for the starter, he pushed all the buttons he could locate. The engine fired and, crashing the gears, he found reverse and then backed towards a minor lane leading to the village, hitting several stationary vehicles en route.

Those villagers living on the periphery of Mirabeau heard the commotion as he carried on, unaware of what was really happening. In his crazy state of mind, he was driving a Renault FT tank along the Rue de Rivoli again. People heard the noise as Philippe steered the excavator into whatever faced him. Not a cottage was without a twitching curtain or a drawn blind.

Philippe thought he had a small cluster of explosives in his pocket. Often he tried to carry a deterrent and Marc was horrified when he discovered Philippe's secret, warning him of instant dismissal if he disobeyed his request to disarm. People tried to use their telephones, but the lines were making strange noises. The mayor's number was permanently engaged. Panic arrived with speed and a crowd began to whisper to each other. Had the Boche returned? Wasn't the war over? An elderly neighbour of Germaine's slashed his throat when shaving, as a feeling of terror and anxiety overwhelmed him.

Marc had difficulty driving into the square, as a mass of people were retreating from the angry machine. In the beam of his headlights he saw it lurching across the lane, miraculously avoiding the deep ditches. Marc's dilemma was whether to attempt to overtake it, slam on the brakes, or follow slowly behind at a distance. His main concern was for Philippe, as intuition told him that he was the driver. Germaine, sitting next to Marc, was anxiously looking in all directions. The lane petered out, the road returning to its original width and surface. Almost at once, Marc knew where Philippe was heading.

The small intimate square of Mirabeau's uneven concrete surface and pockmarked enclosed walls scarred by bullet holes had remained untouched as a reminder of the German atrocities. It had become a source of conflicting arguments – some villagers said that they had no need to be reminded of three years of occupation and many had no desire to have memories of massacres brought alive. The square was in itself a sad memorial to the dead and a meeting place for those lucky enough to still be living.

Marc pulled up behind a wooden seat. The leaves of the plane trees hung limp in the heat, standing as a backdrop to an advancing, darkening sky. For a brief moment, he watched a group of youths running past. His attention returned to Philippe, as the earth-moving machine recklessly crashed into anything in its way. Several buildings had been damaged in its wake. The now silent crowd stood flabbergasted. Most of them had known Philippe all of their lives. From schooldays and through the horrors of war, he had been their overseer in the vineyards, their go-between as bailiff to the Comte. It was Philippe who walked down the lines of fruitful vines with their wages in a heavy bag, the coins jangling. In some cases, he was their confessor, as Father Francis appeared to be out of touch.

The huddled villagers whispered to one another in the gathering groups. 'He's gone mad, he'll kill us all!' The gendarmes in Arles were on strike, sympathising with the postal workers' union. Marc stood several metres from the machine, waving his arms and calling out, but Philippe simply ignored him and continued with his intention to drive into Marc's van. The excavator shunted backwards into a belt of trees, where children had been playing tag.

From behind a clump of bushes, Father Francis appeared, carrying a large wooden crucifix. 'Poor man,' he muttered, 'it has all been too much for him. He has finally broken in mind and spirit.' The priest pushed past Marc. 'I have to administer the last rites to any of the injured who are dying,' he continued. 'Why isn't the mayor here? The police must be informed.'

'Impossible!' Marc replied. 'The village has been cut off as the phone lines have been bulldozed down.'

'You could drive to Arles or Beaucaire and telephone from there,' the priest persisted.

'No, Father, Philippe does not need the law, he needs a doctor and a straitjacket.'

'Do what you think is right, my son,' the priest said. He hurried away towards bodies lying on the ground.

Philippe sat in the cab staring into space. In his crazed mind, all he saw were German soldiers, lying dead. Re-starting the engine, the excavator bumped and lurched forward, leaving the square behind.

Eventually Grich's house came into view. A chilling sound

of hysterical laughter escaped from Philippe's exhausted body. For the deranged man, Grich's house became a Boche blockhouse and home to at least sixty enemy soldiers, who were armed and ready to kill him. He pushed down on the accelerator and lowered the giant bucket scoop.

Hans, sitting in his wilderness of a garden, had been enjoying the feeling of satisfaction that the peace of the gathering twilight brought to him. This was soon to be shattered. His two dogs, sitting by his feet, stood up when the clattering machine appeared, cutting the silence and destroying his magical period of solitude.

In manic disorder, Philippe aimed the excavator towards the ancient house, with the intention to destroy the place, reduce it to a pile of rubble, including the occupants. Similar thoughts had urged him on to destroy Nuage, to erase all the rotten bloody memories that were destroying his mind. Provence was a beautiful dream – so many times Marc had said that, and Philippe's tormented mind still produced these lucid thoughts.

Hans, rooted in his chair in sheer disbelief, suddenly realised his imminent danger. With incredulity, he watched the machine, lurching in undignified spasms of zippy, high-geared motivation, as the engine hiccupped towards him. He knew the giant bulldozer came from Nuage and the driver was possibly the wretched bailiff. A wave of disappointment broke over him, he hoped he had put Philippe out of action – obviously not.

Mad! The stupid old man was completely mad, he deduced. Was anyone sane in this remote primitive land, occupied by ignorant peasants who could hardly read or write? Their one asset was the ability to produce fine wine, which in some places was still made with the help of filthy feet, treading fruit in age-old vats and poured into oak casks. No surprise, Hans thought, that the Führer had been teetotal. Almost unbelievable that his father had become bewitched by this lost land of tribes, who carved out a meagre existence within its unwelcoming, rugged, natural beauty.

161

Philippe guided the killing machine closer into position. Hans, deafened by the noise, tried to calm the terrified dogs. Much of the demolition had already been done as Hans's house was in a sad state of dereliction, aided by sheer neglect and assisted by nature's habit of governing the elements. For too long the place had been abandoned, the damage offering proof of forsaken hope. It had been a refuge for tramps, teenagers, gypsies and Resistance members, who had lived with the odd herd of wild goats and other creatures.

It was all over in seconds. In Philippe's disturbed state, he drove on and the final remaining wall had become Fresnes Prison. Crumbling masonry fell to the ground, filling the air with dust, hitting the guard sitting with his dogs whose loud barking ceased. Philippe was overcome by a wave of success, his aching eyes were filled with dust. He searched for signs of movement. Neither Grich, nor his dogs, were anywhere to be seen.

Exhausted, Philippe laid his aching head on the steering wheel. Marc found him slumped in his cab and lifted his shaking body out. Philippe moaned and spoke. 'Did I get the *salaud*?'

Marc held him in his arms. 'Yes Philippe, you've done a wonderful job. Now, let's get you to a doctor.' Germaine appeared, stumbling over the rubble, and between them they somehow managed to get Philippe into Marc's van.

'Talk to him,' Marc said. 'Keep him busy with nice thoughts.'

'Sexy or old memories?' Germaine asked.

Marc laughed, starting the van's engine. 'Philippe can't still be that active on the sexual front?'

'You don't know Philippe!' She gave a scornful laugh.

'*Au contraire* – I know him very well,' Marc replied.

Again she laughed.

'Well no, not that well. We'll have to take him to the clinic at St Luc,' Marc said.

'In Arles?' she protested.

162

'I don't care if it's at the end of the world, I owe it to
him.'

Philippe remained in the clinic for longer than Marc had
anticipated. The morphine injections induced a variety of
ghosts, past and present, visiting him in the coma, of which
he remembered nothing. Because of his condition, the doctor
had insisted a restraint was attached to his leg, to keep him
secure in the bed. Again, Philippe fell back into the past, as
the restraint became the leg iron that the Nazis had put round
his ankle, chaining him to the cell wall. Being too tight, it
had worn into his skin, the flesh festering and the wound
oozing pus. The doctor ignored his request to have the restraint
removed and he soon found Philippe sitting up in bed,
examining his ankle. Only the scar was there, not having
faded with the memories.

Father Francis visited him once, while Philippe was riding
the waves of consciousness. Sadly, for both of them, the visit
was a bad idea. The priest did not stay for the whole visiting
time allocated, as Philippe's abusive behaviour forced the
nursing staff to escort the priest to the hospital entrance.

During long consultations with the neurosurgeon and
continuous visits of psychiatrists, Marc found sympathy. Always
the same questions were asked and the same answers given,
so the same conclusion was formed.

The patient's psychiatrist looked at him over his spectacles,
his gaze long and understanding. 'Monsieur Coutanche is
suffering more than a head injury, and of course, there is
physical pain – we have to consider his mental state.' He
paused. 'M'sieur le Comte, there are thousands of casualties
like him, suffering from the same problem and that...' he
bent over his notes, 'that includes yourself. This we called
"guilt retribution", but now it is called guilt survival.'

'Why should I feel guilt?' Marc asked.

'Because you and many others are still here.' He sighed. 'I'm afraid it's a natural conclusion and will keep presenting itself to members of my profession. It will keep us employed for a long time into the future. Imagine those who survived the Holocaust – don't you think they suffered guilt too?'

Marc nodded. The doctor was absolutely right. Before he could reply the doctor continued. 'Don't worry. Coutanche will perhaps come through this very regrettable incident and live to tell his grandchildren.'

'They are part of his problem, and mine too,' Marc said, thinking of Marie-Jeanne, the reincarnation of Sylvie, his past love.

'With medication and faith you will both survive.' The doctor picked up his file, indicating that the discussion was over. As Marc drove away, he knew what he had been told was true. His ideal, to share his future with a woman he loved, was a feeling he had lost years ago, in a concrete cell devoid of everything. He now reasoned that where there was life, there was always hope.

The night before his brother arrived, Marc was expected to be on site with the obsequious young man from the Ministry, still arguing his personal point of view. However, he was too preoccupied with the impending arrival of Leo, Karin and Simone's two boys. Charles had been working hard lately and Simone felt Leo needed her support at the factory, so they were both glad of some time together, without their boys. There were still several upstairs rooms Marc needed to get finished, and he had to buy more furniture.

Their arrival was not a noisy one. Both Leo and Karin were aware of the sounds made by heavy machinery as they climbed out of the airport taxi and saw the mess of builders' works. Immediately, Marc noticed how much Simone's sons had grown. They were subdued, remaining shyly in the background. Germaine came out to greet them. It was years since she had seen Leo and Karin was a total stranger. The greetings were long and any repressed excitement was released in the vigorous handshakes and hugs. For a few moments all work on the building stopped, as the workmen laid down tools and stood with straightened backs, staring in disbelief at the restrained 'English' mode of greeting, without the natural warmth of the Gallic embrace at a family reunion.

Marc suggested they have breakfast outside. Relieved, Germaine agreed. Leo had put on weight, Marc noticed, and was looking well and relaxed. Marc suggested to Germaine that she take Piers and Crispin to the crêperie to buy chocolate and exercise Bruno, Philippe's dog. She nodded in approval, as she could check that Marie-Jeanne was all right, able to cope with customers and not burning too many crêpes. The other two young girls who helped during the school holidays were devoid of common sense, prone to breaking cups and glasses, often involving customers who demanded compensation for ruined clothes.

Later, busying himself in his study, Marc waited for Leo. He knew exactly what he was going to say with carefully chosen words. On his desk lay the final accounts of the factory, which Leo had brought with him. Leo entered the study, his steps almost jaunty.

'OK if we get started now?'

Yes,' Marc replied. 'I'll ask Germaine to bring us coffee.'

'She's gone out with the boys.'

'Yes, I forgot. Oh, by the way, the cheque from the buyers of Cheval is in the bank on deposit.'

'The interest won't be much.' Marc said

'I think we've done quite well.'

The factory and all their business concerns had been transferred to a man called Joseph Bleib. Leo had concluded the whole deal, much to Marc's relief.

'Yes, I'm delighted with the result, I'm more than pleased.'

Leo lit a cigarette and walked to the newly-replaced window. 'It was hard work.'

'You're so good with figures, I knew you wouldn't let us down. How's Karin?'

'Karin's very well. We're closer than we've ever been. That doctor she's under has worked on her and my wife is now a new woman, and the biggest miracle of all is that we are going to adopt a baby! Hard to believe, don't you think? We can always blame Simone. Her two boys are a delight.'

Marc stared at him. His face held a puzzled expression. 'What on earth are you saying? Simone has done nothing.'

In disbelief, Marc shook his head. Simone had her reasons for silence.

She had produced two sons, neither of which could bear the name of Chevaud, but he and his brother had not sired any offspring and who knows the history of an intended adopted baby. Leo would pass on his family name but its lineage would probably remain a mystery.

21

Marc had begun to take regular exercise, early in the mornings before the workforce arrived. Noises from jackhammers competed with the sounds of animals in the forest – the jackhammers always won. He loved this place that God had created for him and others who had the good fortune to live here. One word only could describe his surroundings – destruction, with the exception of a large, semi-derelict house. An area of devastation with the remains of a half-renovated house, supported by the metal arms of scaffolding, gazed sadly through the eyes of broken windows to the hills beyond.

His legs aching, he chose a nearby rock to stop and take a brief rest. It was a time he loved more than any other, with dawn breaking over the mountains, their snow-capped peaks greeted pink by a rising sun. Now, he always had a constant companion in the shape of Bruno, who needed the exercise and was grateful for the attention he received. The biscuits the Comte fed him were more appetising than those offered by his master.

Marc had one penultimate hurdle to clear, more complex and time-consuming: further discussions with the advocate he had engaged for the appearance at the Court of War Crimes Commission. It had been explained in lengthy detail what this visit to the tribunal would entail: the enormous amount of files and paperwork that had to be presented in evidence.

The total sum of compensation being asked for was immense. It was not solely for damage which the chateau had suffered, there was also the matter of art theft and many other crimes.

The issue of the priceless pictures caused the greatest shock of all, but it was Marc's father who had the last laugh.

As Marc explained to the residing Magistrate and senior Judge, it was his mother, the late Comtesse, who had been the comptroller of antiquities at Nuage before the war. She was considered an expert and had been a confidante to Van Gogh, Cezanne and Pissarro. Van Gogh had been a guest at the chateau on his frequent visits to Provence, while Cezanne had become a close friend, and his visits were more extended and frequent, becoming less secretive than the artist wished.

Back then, the Comte, Marc's father, on his return from a secret period of absence in Copenhagen, on the pretext of technical work for Germany, asked to see the most recent pictures. With his good sense of investment, plus his excellent eye for beauty, he saw there was potential in the artist's work. He had copies made which were hung in the grand salon and the foyer. The originals were carefully packed and crated, stored behind a wall in a disused still room, where he knew the temperature would be perfect. His masons used old stone from a worked-out quarry to build a false wall. One of his neighbours, a well-known *vigneron*, had done this to his own cellars, hiding rare and vintage wines from the invaders.

During his bouts of madness, Philippe imagined a variety of events, some real, some fantasy. Since he had come home from the clinic, Germaine had become used to his periods of derangement, but on occasion his damaged mind appeared normal. She found it difficult to separate normality from insanity. Releasing the brake on the wheelchair, she pushed it towards the locked French windows and, unlocking them, steered him on to the lawn outside. She sat on the grass by his side. At first, she tried making general conversation, uncertain whether he understood her words. Suddenly he began to talk of pictures.

'What pictures?' she asked scathingly. 'You know the Boche took the ones from the chateau.'

'Nothing of the kind, you know nothing, woman! I know what I'm saying. I *have* to speak to the Seigneur. Telephone him now!' He paused for breath. She saw a dribble from his mouth run down his unshaven chin.

'Not a word to anyone,' he continued, 'except M'sieur Marc, understand?

'All right,' she muttered irritably. 'I'll go now. Do you want to stay here to watch the birds and bees?'

'Yes,' he answered, 'don't let anyone see you.'

'It's nearly time for lunch,' she said. 'Are you hungry?'

'*Normalment,*' he replied, turning his head to watch her hurried departure.

Marc had planned to spend the afternoon sifting through accounts, ledgers and bulging files of official papers. Locking himself away with a bottle of cognac and a fresh box of cigars, he hardly had time to settle in a comfortable chair before a series of quiet tapping noises on the door disturbed his tired and anxious mind.

Germaine stood on the threshold, her mouth tight over drawn lips.

'I hope this is urgent, Germaine,' he said. 'I've enough work to last me forever.'

'May I speak with you?' She took a faltering step forward. 'I apologise for disturbing you, but I assure you it is most important that I speak and you listen to what I have to say.'

He pulled open the heavy door, allowing her to come into the room.

'Sit down,' he said.

'It's Philippe. He's getting worse and delirious, insisting he sees you and you alone.'

'About what?' Marc asked.

She shook her head and raised her arms, waiving them in a desperate gesture. 'He's rattling on about an old still room, and calling the masons Nazi robbers. I don't know what to do.'

Marc poured a measure of brandy for her. 'Here, drink this, it will do you good.' He paused to replace the cork in the bottle. 'It appears he's getting worse. Perhaps it is time he was readmitted to the clinic on a permanent basis. That still room, is it used now?'

'Not since your father left. Your dear mother used it for her flowers and there were times when Remy and others produced *marc*. After that Frie business, maybe you should let the builders pull it down, like they did with the old washhouse.' She sipped her brandy as he noticed how her hand was trembling. 'After Frie, who knows what we will find? More dead bodies, more skeletons in the cupboard?'

'That's enough, Germaine,' he said. There was anger in his voice.

'M'sieur?' She asked.

'Never mind.' He stood to stretch his legs, 'Is he awake?'

She shrugged her shoulders. 'Who can tell?' She spoke with her back to him. 'Sometimes he talks rubbish, on other days he makes sense. He has terrible nightmares. It must be connected with the past. You know I can't believe half of what he says. It is too repulsive.' She half turned to face him. 'M'sieur, what did happen to him?'

Marc spoke softly. 'You don't want to know, it is beyond belief. Ready to go now? I'll talk to Philippe – maybe we shall get some sense out of him.'

'Maybe,' she replied.

Their walk to see Philippe was slow, each deep in thought. It crossed Marc's mind that perhaps he should now tell Germaine about his becoming an uncle again. Germaine was not impressed, and gave a harrumphed exclamation.

Philippe appeared to be sleeping peacefully. Marc took an

old wooden chair from the kitchen and sat in the shade next to Philippe.

'What's up, old chap? Are you in pain?'

Philippe moaned, '*Mon Seigneur*, I have to say what is on my mind. Are we alone?'

'Absolutely!' Marc replied.

'Where is that bitch of a Gestapo guard?' Philippe's confusion was alarming.

'I strangled her.' Marc said, playing along with Philippe's fantasy.

'That's too good for her. Did you hit her with a bottle like I did to that fascist Frie?'

'Now, I believe you have something to tell me, Philippe?'

Suddenly Philippe moved his bandaged head to look at Marc. He spoke lucidly and began to relate how he and the late Comte had lovingly wrapped and crated the great art treasures, before storing them in the old still room, behind a false wall which Remy and other employees had built, using genuine old stone from the nearby abandoned quarry. By the time they had finished, the result was so perfect, it tied in with the original centuries-old walls.

Quite unexpectedly, Philippe burst out laughing. It was an unnerving sound. 'Don't you see?' he said, 'they are all there! You must save them before the saboteurs begin to dynamite the walls.' He stopped and his mind drifted. 'My favourite is the one that man Caesar did of your mother.'

'I don't remember that one very well,' Marc said.

'You wouldn't, she kept it locked away from your father.'

'Are you certain it was Caesar?' Impatiently Marc began to wish the visit would end, as he realised Philippe was confusing Cezanne, the artist, with Caesar, the Roman Emperor. He decided to let it go. How could anyone argue with a confused and demented person? 'Surely, the Boche stole all the pictures?' Marc said.

Again, Philippe laughed. 'That's what they *thought*, but

171

with the Commandant's diplomas in art, he was like the pictures he stole, all fakes! Your papa was a very clever man. Now you see, I could only speak to you.'

'Before the labourers go in there with their picks and shovels, we will need help.' Marc stood up. 'I have to go now Philippe, it's time for the prison roll-call and that mess they call dinner.' Cleverly, he had played along with the injured man and this acting had achieved some success. In his mind he was not certain as to which words were authentic and which were fantastic images, manufactured in a damaged brain now tainted by incoherent monomaniacal memories of sadistic interludes, which degraded any human being and could never be forgotten or erased.

Philippe's left hand clutched at the sheet. 'More cabbage soup and black bread! I'm not hungry.'

'À demain,' Marc said, and left the room, his heart heavy with sadness, encased in a feeling of desolation. Deciding to co-opt Germaine into his plan to discover if Philippe had spoken the truth, he asked her to accompany him back to Nuage.

To his aggravation and annoyance, he saw a figure of a man standing in the centre of the inner courtyard, deep in conversation with Remy. It seemed to him that they would never have the opportunity to be allowed to do what he had planned. Sent from Paris, the official stopped his conversation and turned to see Marc approaching. He held a large folder of documents regarding the chateau in his hand. Using the folder as a pointer, he said, his voice almost aggressive, '*That* wall is not safe and will have to come down. It needs to be rebuilt with iron strengtheners.' Using the folder again as a pointer, he added, 'And *those* steps, where do they lead?'

Marc began to walk away, the surveyor's words lost in the noise of workmen's tools. Together, he and Germaine went to Marc's van, got in and drove off at an alarming speed.

172

* * *

The next day, Marc bolted the kitchen door behind him before going to find Germaine. Suggesting she go with him to the still room, without hesitation she stopped preparing the vegetables for their next meal and followed him.

The still room was perhaps just over twelve metres long and, in keeping with the rest of the chateau, was built of local stone. Old granite sinks lined one wall, home for a multitude of spiders who had become imprisoned in their own webs. Shelves packed with stone jars and empty glass bottles towered above blackened copper pans, veiled in cobwebs. A giant pulping machine waited silently for a fresh consignment of grape skins, complete with seeds, to be crushed beneath worn stone rollers.

Leo had joined them. Full of curiosity, his voice broke the silence.

'What is this place?' he asked. 'It feels like a vault. Cold enough too. Was it an old wash-house?'

'No,' Marc replied, lifting the rusty handle of the press, causing it to squeal. 'It was for *marc*.'

'You're talking in riddles!' Leo said, his voice in an exasperated tone.

Marc sighed. 'You know Leo, it's a shame that I've lived in France more than you. It's time I taught you a few things, then you could say you were a true Provençal.'

'Yes, perhaps you should,' came Leo's reply.

'*Marc* is a drink,' his brother continued. 'A very potent beverage made from the pomace of grapes. On occasions in the past it has been declared illegal.'

'You mean like absinthe? It made people blind?'

'Possibly blind drunk, Leo. Papa stopped the process as the workers became too tipsy to do their jobs properly. Production of high quality wine fell drastically.'

'I expect he had a strike on his hands,' Leo said dryly.

'Our men were too loyal, they just enjoyed messing about the Boche, by producing base alcohol when they were forced to work for the Nazis without pay.'

'Why are we down here?' Leo asked.

'Inspecting the place. The wall behind you is due for demolition.' Marc hesitated, unsure whether to continue. 'When that happens, all shall be revealed.'

'All or perhaps nothing.'

Marc turned his head, seeking Germaine's silent agreement, but she had tactfully left them, with her intention to fetch Remy, who earlier had been asked by Marc to start demolishing the wall.

'Ah, here he comes,' Marc said, raising a hand in greeting.

'I took time off to visit Philippe,' Remy explained. 'He is not too good.'

Germaine reached out to take the adze Remy held. 'I clean my vegetable plot with one of these,' she said 'You're going to need something much heavier, try a pickaxe.'

'Too risky,' Remy replied.

'Let's get on with it,' Marc said. 'I'd like you to swear your complete secrecy of all that may happen here today.' He hoped he had not offended them, by possibly hinting at doubting their loyalty.

There was the sound of assent. Marc knew his employees and former colleagues could be totally trusted. Their courage during the numerous episodes of cruel interrogation they had suffered proved their loyalty.

Remy took two steps to face Marc, offering the adze. 'It is right for you to take the first swing.'

Marc shook his head, 'No!' he declared. 'That we leave for you, Remy.' He patted his arm. 'Good luck.'

Remy pulled at a loose stone and others followed it to the floor, sending up a thick cloud of sandy dust. His strong hands grasped more bits of rocky stone and he pulled, tugged and twisted them until they were loose. When a hole appeared, big enough for his satisfaction, he called out, 'Someone pass me a torch!' His words were lost in the dark void ahead of him. The dust and the darkness hurt his sore eyes.

After a long pause, he called. 'There is something here.'

'Take care,' Marc warned. 'You don't know what's in there.'

22

Germaine had expressed no surprise at Marc's announcement that a VIP would be arriving that day and it would be nice to give them a true Provençal lunch. Her final words were to complain about Philippe's condition and apparent slow recovery. It was her opinion that Philippe needed a permanent carer or a qualified nurse to help her cope more efficiently. Many of her duties were being neglected, she sadly reflected, a fact that Marc had noticed, usually with feelings of guilt, and Germaine secretly admitted to herself that she could no longer cope.

Marie-Jeanne was young and not conversant with nursing a disabled man. Nor was she willing to take her grandfather to the toilet. Her youth magnified her embarrassment.

'Leave it with me,' Marc said to Germaine. 'We'll sort out his care soon. Did you find any champagne anywhere?'

She nodded. 'Yes, Remy's gone with Marie-Jeanne to Arles, but they'll pay a fortune for one bottle!'

The shrill ringing of a telephone in the study summoned him. A woman's voice seductively spoke, confirming a meeting with him the next day. She spoke quickly, with a Parisian accent. It was further news from the Ministry, which meant nothing to him. During the past months there must have been hundreds of officials calling to inspect, direct, or give instructions. Why did he bother? Was the whole project worth the enormous effort? Perhaps he should forget the whole idea and leave his ambitious dreams to fade into nothing. These thoughts rang true. As a postscript, the caller added that she had a substantial cheque for him.

Madelaine Fournier understood the word 'perfection'. She had been lucky throughout the war and had managed to keep a good wardrobe, despite shortages and rationing. Her present position at the Musée des Peintures, Paris, in such a prestigious place, meant her vast knowledge of her subject was ultimately recognised. The status she had achieved in the Jeu de Paumes, close to the Louvre, was evidence of the way she was respected as an indomitable character, by the Germans and their superiors. She had been the victim of malicious gossip, based on the necessity of working closely with the occupying forces. In their eyes, she was a collaborator, but they freely admitted their lack of informed knowledge of famous French artists.

One Major, however, became besotted by her. Terrified of probable consequences, she had to be extremely careful and always on her guard. Fear of reprisals from her own compatriots could create difficult situations with the German authorities. The hierarchy frowned upon fraternisation with French women; even prostitutes had to be vetted. In her case, the Major held the whip hand, with no desire to dismiss her from her coveted post or permit his advances to finish.

She hated the thought of having her gorgeous auburn hair chopped off and her head shaved, the fate of so many women accused of collaborating. Fortunately for her, there were several among her circle of academics and artistic colleagues (some Resistance members) who were loyal, and their trust was made known to the Allies on the liberation of Paris.

The Jeu de Paumes had been possessed by a special unit, with orders and carefully chosen men, supervised by Hermann Göring. Looted valuables from all over France were kept there and meticulous details carefully filed away.

Her apartment was in a fashionable street by the Tuilleries. It was a spacious flat off the Rue de Rivoli, which, before the war, had been a high-class area of residences. There was a front terrace, furnished with garden seats and ornaments depicting heroes of Greek mythology. In the summer, a bevy of scarlet geraniums brushed the granite flagstones with fallen petals.

Her lineage was nothing special. Her family were not wealthy or known for heroic deeds. One important facet of their character was the respect they had earned. Her father, a professor of French history at the Sorbonne, was well known for his outspoken views and his political opinions. It was due to his associating with Marxists that the Gestapo arrested him. When his disappearance caused concern, she was in her mid-twenties. An honorary title was conferred on her by the Sorbonne and her German employers were aware she had access to information of what was happening at the university. Because of her father, a suspect on the Nazis blacklist, she too was watched and sometimes followed.

Ironically, it was her German Major who saved her from arrest. He stressed how important her position was and Göring relied on her judgement of paintings. The implication was strong, with the Germans believing she was close to the Field Marshall and possibly Herr Hitler too.

The race to get to Paris was a muddled period. De Gaulle wanted to be President, the communists sought power and the Allies wanted neither. Most of Eastern Europe was controlled by red governments. Most people, German or others, knew it was all wishful thinking. Paris was in turmoil. There was anarchy, with no semblance of a government; Berlin was a sea of rubble and devastation spread out over acres of what had been Hitler's pride and joy.

Peacetime was a climax, she told herself. The bad old days were over, never to return. It was the Americans who helped rekindle the fires of burning, impassioned memories. Activities gradually returned to the city, whose inhabitants had been starved for so long of culture and leisurely pursuits. The sound of traditional jazz echoed along the left bank, couples danced into the night, or were taught to jive by GIs on the cobbled streets.

Once more, the boulevards of Paris welcomed lovers, and

the plane trees enticed them down to the banks of the Seine, where they gave and received stolen kisses, with breath freshened by Dentyne chewing-gum. Fresh drops of rain fell from a sky clear of aeroplanes and free from falling bombs, cooling the heat of the night. It was possible to sense the excitement of overjoyed people on an August evening. No one cared if it rained or snowed. Women who had tolerated hardships for years had grudgingly accepted female deprivations – shoe polish as replacement mascara, and a dye painted on bare legs, replacing real nylons. Eventually, silk stockings were readily replaced by generous American soldiers, a commodity they always seemed to have in plentiful supply.

Because of her qualifications and CV, having recently become a Professor herself, Madelaine was invited to join the staff at the Jeu de Paumes. It was an order she happily obeyed – helping to trace looted treasure was exciting. Her knowledge of the French Impressionists was awesome and when it was suggested she visit Provence, she jumped at the chance. The trip, she decided, was initially to Brittany, where she would walk the quaysides of Pont Aven, soaking up the atmosphere and sharing the magical scenes of an ambiance Van Gogh and Cézanne had loved so much.

Her break in Brittany was far too short, and the ensuing journey by train gave the opportunity to catch up on paperwork. Her supervisor in Paris had given her complete freedom, with a generous expense account. Bruised by a tranche of cunningness, learned from the wounds of war and terror, she had decided to milk her situation, and make up for lost time and opportunities that a young painter had missed. Her last vacation had been back in 1938, when she accompanied her father to London for a symposium at the university. She had been happy to follow him, and visit the galleries that had remained with open doors for concerts and entertainment, but devoid of works of art, safely hidden away in worked-out quarries in Wales, in anticipation of war.

To Madelaine's surprise, Arles had not altered very much, as Vichy had escaped with a minor portion of war damage. The grandeur of the medieval buildings and Roman ruins could still be felt in the incredible examples of classical architecture. Magnificent small shops had been emptied of souvenirs. The shop windows had only held a scattering of cheap shoddy wooden toys, displayed to tempt the Wehrmacht soldiers, as they ventured into Vichy France during the war.

The local residents had altered, adopting suspicious expressions for strangers, and each other in some cases. They had realised how gullible they had been to trust old army General Pétain in his dotage, whose senility and death were not far away, in the pay of the Nazis who smirked behind his back. Most of the suffering was horrific and genuine. In Vichy things were different. The Milice, under Nazi control, consisted of French males and some women too. A civil war and a second reign of terror was reminiscent of another revolution of over a century before.

Her dark glasses were not strong enough against the blazing sun. She walked towards a cab rank – there were just two vacant taxis. After the drivers had stopped arguing over which one would take her fare, she got into one, sat back on the worn leather seat and looked at the comprehensive list she had made of places to be investigated. It was not alphabetical but geographical, and Mirabeau was just over thirty kilometres from Arles. She kicked off her shoes and began to relax.

23

During the time Marc spent walking his estate, he enjoyed the peace and valued the private moments shared with the dog. It seemed his problems were too numerous, as each day produced new ones with new difficulties, some unsolvable. The completion of Nuage seemed never-ending. Once he had accepted that the project was compensatory, things did begin to change for the better. The sale of Cheval Zips had been successful and profitable, with Leo's help, who had surprised Marc with his ability to haggle.

Marc thanked God for the remarkable change in his brother's miserable life. Karin too had blossomed into a likeable woman. He made a note of the psychiatrist she had seen, a reminder that if he ever personally needed help in that area, he would consult the same doctor.

Philippe caused the biggest headache of all. Marc knew he had to resolve the problem concerning his bailiff. It was not going to be an easy job. Philippe was a stubborn old goat, his present disability making him more cantankerous than ever. Being confined to a bed or a wheelchair brought frustrations to him and those who loved him. They wished to share his agony, but they too experienced wounds, theirs being of a mental nature, whereas Philippe suffered physical pain too.

Marc knew that the key to the solution was in Germaine's hands – she was the one who could handle Philippe and Marie-Jeanne. The girl had become useful as a caring adult and, while living under difficult conditions, was quick to learn.

The rock on which he had been resting became cold and damp. Marc slid off, startling Bruno, and together they headed back to Nuage where Germaine was waiting for him.

Protected by a fresh navy-blue *tablier*, Germaine was coming out of the builders' hut, which was being used as a site office. Her face showed relief when she saw the loping gait of Bruno.

'I've missed him,' she said, 'and Philippe said the beast has not had any breakfast!'

'Do you mean Philippe?' Marc asked her.

'No,' she replied. 'He has had breakfast at five this morning. I've tidied round as best I could. I wish these plasterers would leave their boots outside before they come in here. Can't you see to them outside? Marie-Jeanne has gone with Remy to Beaucaire for fresh supplies – I need aubergines.'

'Why bother to tidy this place?'

'I spend my life tidying,' she complained. 'You'll have to entertain outside. It's a nice day.'

'Whatever,' he said, bored now.

'You sound a bit down,' she remarked. 'What's wrong?'

'Everything,' he complained. 'Where's my brother?'

'Taken his wife and the boys to the market.' She went to wipe a smeared window. A taxi had arrived so she made her way to the door. 'You'd better have a shave,' she suggested. 'They may take you for Bluebeard!' She left him to receive their guest.

Madelaine was not surprised at the mess. Sadly, she had witnessed many other buildings in a similar state, but the sight of Nuage was a fresh introduction to man's aggression and incomprehensible violence. She had seen many photos and plans, held at the office. Nuage, once an example of outstanding architectural elegance, was now a catastrophic example of mayhem. Her hand shaking from anger, she held out her visiting card and Germaine noticed that there were no rings on her fingers.

'Mademoiselle, M'sieur le Comte is expecting you, but a little later.'

Madelaine apologised quietly and smiled. 'I can easily wait outside and enjoy the sun.'

Germaine opened the main house door wide. 'Please come in,' she ushered Madelaine into the grand vestibule, their footsteps muffled by the protective sheeting covering the newly laid marble floor. Madelaine's experienced eyes saw how magnificent it had once been and she wondered why or how the invaders could succumb to such wanton destruction and obscene vandalism. Swiftly she followed Germaine through a series of passages to a courtyard at the rear of the site. Sidestepping the building debris was like crossing a minefield.

Marc changed quickly, replacing working clothes for a light green suit, with a pale blue shirt and red tie. He slipped on leather loafers and pulled out a silk handkerchief in his top pocket, sorting it to his satisfaction, before meeting his official guest, and wondering how she would differ from all the fussy bureaucrats he had had the misfortune to entertain. While swallowing his pride, he was diplomatically requesting money, grants to cover cost of restoration of his family home. Before he opened the door of his hastily tidied study, he had already formed a mental picture of the visitor from Paris: thick spectacles, small in stature, short, straight, black hair, possibly with a fringe, giving the impression of a medieval page. Professor-types he had met before: at the Sorbonne or maybe in a remote prison somewhere.

Overcome by his wrong assessment, he approached her with an extended hand. She was tall, with a provocative angle of her hips accentuating her bodyline, on to which his eyes seemed fixed.

'I am sorry to have kept you waiting.' He slipped his hand that had been shaking hers into a trouser pocket. She smiled, forming a wide mouth.

'It should be me apologising,' she said, and smiled again. He noticed her perfect teeth and could smell her perfume.

'May I offer you an aperitif or some coffee?' he asked, lifting a small brass bell on the desk.

'Coffee,' she replied, turning round to see Germaine enter.

'Some coffee please, Germaine,' Marc ordered and, without speaking, Germaine went back to her cooking.

Marie-Jeanne burst in to the kitchen with a bag of groceries. 'You will die when you hear what we had to pay for the champagne!' she said, dropping the shopping on to the scrubbed tabletop.

'Take this coffee into monsieur's study, please. His visitor is here. Then cycle back home and take Philippe a mug and check his sheets, they may be wet.'

Marc suggested Madelaine sit down while she drank her coffee. 'My housekeeper has been busy preparing a traditional Provençal lunch, which we can enjoy outside.'

She smiled over the rim of her cup. 'It smells delicious,' she remarked, 'it's a cuisine I do not know.'

He tutted playfully, returning her smile. 'We shall have to educate you. Our culinary offerings can be devastating. I trust you are not a vegetarian?'

She shook her head, the loose curls around her ears playing with her sapphire earrings. She should have had emeralds, he thought, to match the colour of her eyes.

'I think we should go outside,' he said, looking at his watch. 'Lunch will be ready quite soon.'

'May I wash my hands?' she asked.

'Yes, of course.' He rang the bell again, and this time Marie-Jeanne answered, breathlessly.

'There is no need to run, Marie-Jeanne,' he scolded.

'I had to go to the cottage, to see if Grandpère was comfortable.'

He sat back in his chair to look at her. 'Tell Germaine we'll be ready for lunch in ten minutes. Meanwhile, please show Mademoiselle Fournier to a place where she can wash her hands.'

Marie-Jeanne nodded. 'Mademoiselle, please come with me, and be careful, it is a dangerous place where we need to go.'

Madelaine stood, brushing her skirt free of imaginary crumbs, and they left the study. Marc picked up *Le Monde* but could not concentrate. He chastised himself for being so easily influenced by Madelaine's good looks. It was a long time since he had felt such a strong frisson when alone with an attractive woman. He made a mental note to dig around for information on Madelaine Fournier. He reminded himself that she was clever and a highly educated woman. She had been in charge of art treasures in Paris for the whole of the occupation, and had worked closely with Göring, who considered himself an art expert and connoisseur. Marc wanted to know all the facts and he knew he would have to tread carefully with Madelaine Fournier.

The obstacle course to find a 'loo' was a nightmare, but Madelaine washed her hands and, to her surprise, hot water flowed from a modern tap. She felt overcome by the strong smell of adhesive used to tile the room, so it was more than refreshing to go and sit outside at a wrought-iron table, beneath a bright yellow parasol. The table had been meticulously prepared with nothing out of place or forgotten. She opened her napkin and laid it across her lap.

The meal was certainly different! Madelaine sipped her wine from a crystal goblet and liked the taste. 'We shall have to get down to the reason why I'm here,' she said, chewing and wondering what she was eating.

'Do you have another site to inspect?'

'No, not yet. They are not ready.'

Finishing her entrée, she laid down her cutlery and allowed Marc to pour more wine into her glass. 'Perhaps a walk around your estate would be more beneficial.'

Laughing, he added more wine to his own glass, and she saw that he was drinking red; hers was a tongue-tingling white.

He had changed his mind over the choice of champagne – that was for later.

'My estate consists of 3,000 hectares. It would take valuable time, which I am sure you do not have. However, you are quite correct, we should tour the house. It is the paintings where your expertise is needed.'

She nodded in agreement and, after enjoying the well prepared food and stimulating conversation, Marc stood and helped Madelaine rise from her chair.

From the beginning, he knew it would not be easy to show her the paintings. Benoit and Remy had placed several wooden tables in the centre of the disused still room, where Marc took her, ready for the grand viewing. She was carrying files, notebooks and a camera. As he lifted each painting to show her, she went to help him and was amazed at their condition. When all eight pictures had been lined up, protected by sheeting against supporting wooden boxes, she gave a series of gasps and could barely conceal her shock and excitement.

Stopping at the first one, she placed a finger on the gilt frame and then took a large magnifying glass to the image. Slowly, with deliberation, she studied it, hardly able to believe her eyes. She spoke into the microphone of a portable tape-recorder, giving the description he had hoped to hear.

'A genuine Pissarro,' she said. 'This is typical of his preference to paint landscapes in sunlight; I believe these are of the Impressionist school.'

'And they are?' he asked.

'Monet and Renoir, and Degas was also, up to a point,' she replied.

'What about Van Gogh and Gauguin?'

She smiled. 'Ah, the Post-Impressionists. You're forgetting Cézanne. In my humble opinion, he was the best, followed by Degas.'

The next set of paintings collection were ten in number. Madelaine took her time and he watched how careful she was, admiring her artistic hands. Finally, she said, 'I'm sorry to tell you that this one by Van Gogh is a fake. It has his signature but the brushwork is all wrong. See how he used colour for its emotive appeal. Of course,' she continued, 'he was here in Provence for some time, until he fell out with Gauguin.'

'What a group of people!' he remarked.

'Yes. A lunatic, a discontented clerk and a dwarf with sexual inadequacies. All in their own way brilliant artists, but I regret to tell you some of these are fake.'

Holding one up, she said, 'This one mystifies me. I can't place it at all. It's definitely a Cézanne. He was born in Aix, a true Proveneux. I cannot identify his model. He always used the same one. This one is unusual. Do you know who this is?'

Marc looked over her shoulder. 'Yes,' he whispered. Almost mesmerised he stroked the picture. 'Yes, I knew her very well.'

'Was she a local girl? Madelaine asked.

'Oh yes, definitely. Her name was Antonia Chevaud, Comtesse of Mirabeau.'

Before the revelation had any impact on her confused mind, she said, 'She was very beautiful, such a kind face.'

'Yes,' he murmured, 'she was lovely.'

'So you knew her? With that name, was she a relation?'

'She was my mother,' he said, with a lump in his throat. 'And I adored her.'

'She knew Cézanne?' Bewildered, Madelaine began to carefully cover the pictures with their protective wrapping.

'Yes, she was fond of him. He was a regular guest here at Nuage. I believe they were lovers.'

'You and I must talk,' she said. 'There's much to do. I'd value this at about $155,000, plus.'

'It is not for sale,' he replied.

'The rest should be auctioned, preferably in New York, as

187

the Americans have the money,' she said. 'You are going to be a very rich man.'

He was emotional to the point of fighting back tears.

Instinctively she felt he needed comforting. Beside her was an anxious and unhappy man. Many others in his position would have wept tears of joy.

'May I ask you a personal question?' she said.

'Yes.'

'Is there a Comtesse now?'

'No.'

'Do you have a wife?'

'No, I've never married. The war put an end to all that.'

'Yes,' she replied, taking his hand. 'The war changed many things, not just people.'

He took her fingers and squeezed them gently. A surge of confidence ran through him; there was a huge sense of rapport.

'Will you have dinner with me, this evening?' he asked.

'I'd like that very much because we can talk.'

'No more words,' he said, raising her hand to his lips. 'Forgive me.'

24

Slowly, silently, they walked away, stumbling over broken stones and the scattered mess the builders had left. It gave Marc a chance and a genuine excuse to help Madelaine when she stumbled in the early evening darkness. Feelings of well-being filled him.

Madelaine felt as if she were in a dream. It was not just the experience of inspecting masterpieces that had elated her – she was alive in an almost make-believe wonderland. Dark days of horror were left behind, perhaps never to be forgotten, but all the time the evil belonged to yesterday. Today was new and in a few hours would become tomorrow. No one knew about the next day. Time would change, like people who could help to alter situations and decisions. Had she not left Paris in 1944 to work for the liberation forces, she might have gone to Germany with the Major. However, when the Americans arrived, the Major ran away and her happiness was complete – she was free!

Marc took her to a bistro in the Cours Lavantre in Beaucaire, his favourite local eating place where he and Philippe had regularly eaten in the past. Armand, the patron, knew him well as a good customer. He stocked Nuage wine and welcomed them with genuine pleasure.

'Monsieur le Comte. *J'espére tu va bien.*' He studied Madelaine.

'*Merci,*' Marc replied. '*Une table profonde.*'

Armand smiled. '*Privé, bien sur. Venez-moi.*' He ushered them to a corner table laid for two, hovering discreetly while Madelaine slipped off her lightweight jacket, which he took from her.

It was a perfect evening, Madelaine thought. Marc hoped it would never end. She was amazed at this different way of life, not just because it was all strange to her, but because it meant complete freedom from Paris; the noise, the traffic, and a thousand other kinds of interruptions. She found Marc easy to talk to, and a good listener.

Several empty wine bottles stood on their table. He decided they had both had enough. Refusing cognac with their coffee, he sat back to survey the scene he was finding so enchanting, and this young woman who had entered his life just a few hours before, who was the cause of his complete contentment.

A thought had occupied her mind for a while, so after a few moments she spoke. 'Tell me,' she said. 'What was your war like? It must have been quiet and reasonably normal, quite different from Paris.'

He laughed and lit a cheroot.

'It was definitely not quiet, but of course, we were too scared to open our mouths, due to all the traitors in the Milice. They were "*salauds*". Excuse me, but they were, and still are. Paris was a hell-hole.'

She wished she had not asked the question and hoped he would not follow, as she knew he was upset.

'And you?' he said, waving a hand to disperse smoke from the cheroot.

'I am as bitter as you obviously are. My father was taken away in a lorry to God knows where.'

In complete disbelief, he stared at her. 'You're Jewish!' he exclaimed in astonishment.

'Heavens no.' She played with a spent cork. 'My father was a devout Catholic with communist associations.'

'That's difficult to understand,' he replied. 'They are diametrically opposed. As a Catholic, I find that hard to believe.'

'It's true,' she said. 'Do you have family?'

'Yes. I have a married sister with two sons who live in England. My brother is here with his wife and my sister's boys, just for a holiday. They are due to return to the UK in about a week. It all rests with you and your boss's decision to pay me in compensation for war damage.'

'It's not up to my superiors. It will be the Germans who are responsible.'

'I shall make arrangements for a trip to London. Will you help me?'

'To do what?' she asked.

'To arrange for some pictures to go for auction. I need expert advice and opinion.'

'Who better to give them to you, but myself? I'd be honoured to be involved in a sale of your masterpieces, but I'd have to have permission to be absent from Paris. There is so much work left for me to do.'

'Thank you,' he said, pushing back his chair. 'Shall we go now?'

It was a typical Mediterranean night, warm, evocative and welcoming. Automatically, he took her arm as they entered a side street and stopped by the parked car.

'I shall have to find a hotel,' she said. 'Or is there a late train to Paris?'

Playfully, he squeezed her arm and she laughed. 'No need for a hotel,' he said. 'There's plenty of room at Nuage and all the beds are new. We can even find you an en-suite.'

She was grateful for the darkness, as it hid her smile of acceptance.

Arriving back in Nuage, he took her arm and they walked slowly to the main door of the chateau. It had all been so perfect; it was unthinkable that it had to end. He found himself wishing the interlude would continue forever. His feelings of loneliness, abandonment, anger and hatred, and the immense mixture of emotions which had smouldered deep inside him, burst into an eagerness for this woman. She not only fascinated him, but her magnetism drew him to passionate thoughts and feelings.

Thoughtfully, Germaine had already turned on the outside light. He led Madelaine to the entrance porch, half hidden by a large urn filled with evergreen plants. In the shadows, he found the courage he had lost, put his arms on her shoulders and bent to kiss her. To his surprise, she turned her head slightly so that his lips touched hers and not her cheek. Her gesture told him that she wanted him to embrace her. It was, for her too, the denouement.

'Thank you,' she said quietly. 'It has been a lovely evening and such an excellent meal.'

He allowed his hands to remain on her shoulders. 'I'm pleased you like our Provençal cuisine. Tomorrow, I should like to take you to Marseille. It is a city of delight, a true picture of France.' He paused. 'I thank you for your company, your helpful advice and your thoroughness in the inspection of my paintings.'

'That was an honour,' she replied. 'A momentous occasion. A one-off which will never be forgotten.'

He released her, reaching forward to open the door.

'Germaine will show you a completed guest room. Shall we find her?'

He did not sleep well, his mind occupied with a multitude of plans and thoughts for the chateau. He had no need to worry, he knew what he intended to do. The biggest thought was the comparison he kept making between Sylvie and Madelaine. It was some time before he realised that his thoughts were not concerning his love for Sylvie. The truth was stark, there were so many differences. He fell asleep going over the conversation of the evening which he had enjoyed with Madelaine; the meal, her clothes, her perfume, her general appearance, her wit. Silently, he scolded himself like a schoolboy in love. Would tomorrow ever come?

25

Germaine and Philippe also had a pleasant evening. She had
sensed the frisson between Marc and the Professor and was
filled with excitement. Marc had had a rough, hazardous
journey through life and he deserved peace of mind and
kindness. As Germaine expounded her feelings to Philippe,
while sitting him on the bed, he held her hand in the darkness
and suddenly she felt relief.

'I told him that he needed a woman,' Philippe said
emphatically. 'Do you think she's the right one?'

'Who knows?' She stroked his bare arm. 'He can be hard
to please. This one is different, special. She has poise and
charm, she will make a beautiful Comtesse.'

'Hey, steady woman. Don't jump to conclusions; it might
be a flash in the pan.'

'He has been alone a long time, I don't want him to be
hurt any more. He's a good man and deserves some security
and love,' Germaine said.

Philippe sighed. 'Don't we all?'

'It's time for my bed,' she said, getting off the bed. 'I've
a lot of work to do. Hard work. The next few days are
going to be difficult with the Professor and the family here.
And the house is still a terrible mess. Why Marc agreed to
their coming, I can't understand. But who am I to say? I just
work here.'

'Don't you see, Germaine?' Philippe said. 'It is all to do
with money. They have sold the business in England to pay
for this place.'

'Won't he get money from the government?' she asked.

'I doubt if it would be enough. That woman you have taken a liking to, she's also from the government.'

'We'll see,' Germaine said. 'I'm off to bed. I've emptied your bottle, now don't miss the hole again. I've enough beds to make at Nuage without you having another accident.'

'I'm sorry,' he said. 'Do you think I enjoy being as I am? Were I not disabled I'd have been out of this bed in seconds and might even pull you in here with me.'

'That will be the day,' she remarked, straightening the covers.

'Yes, and it will come, so you'd best look out!'

She hurried out, a smile of triumph on her face.

Madelaine slept very well, relaxed beneath her duvet, her tired body sinking into the luxury of a good mattress. It seemed as if the fears she felt before leaving Paris had no foundation. So far, it had been rather eventful. The discovery of the art treasures sent thrills through her. They were amazing – no one would believe her. Her boss in the office would think she had lost her mind. Had this episode been a fanciful dream? Fantasy or reality, she had to control any doubts or feelings.

The Comte was interesting, enigmatic, yet he appeared to behave always as a perfect gentleman. His unexpected kiss had taken her breath away, and she experienced astonished happiness now, after a long time. Yesterday was long ago. Replaced by today and there was always tomorrow.

Germaine left the kitchen to see if Philippe needed anything, leaving Leo gazing out of a window. Madelaine was walking across the newly laid gravel, a shaggy dog following her. Leo turned as Marc came into the kitchen.

'Aren't you going to tell me who the gorgeous figure is?' Leo asked.

'What figure?' Marc replied.

'Who is the fabulous creature out there? Don't tell me you've got yourself a woman?'

Marc joined him. 'She is here to value a few articles that the Germans did not pilfer.'

'Yes, but who is she? I did not ask you *what* she is.'

'Fournier is a professor from Paris, an expert in art.'

'Is she staying here?' Leo asked.

Sighing, Marc replied, 'Yes, for a short time. You have no idea of the work we have to get through.'

Leo turned round to face him. 'What sort of work? You and I have a good bit to sort out.'

'Absolutely,' Marc said. 'Let's make a start.' It was almost time for lunch. Marc asked for sandwiches to be brought.

Later that day, Marc, Leo and Karin were outside watching the men working on the west turret. It was amusing to see them climbing up the scaffolding, and swinging on the metal girders, resembling monkeys at the zoo.

They were enjoying an aperitif, but Karin found the extended conversation on financial matters of little concern to her. Marc had explained to her that she was very much involved, due to the plans he had described to his brother regarding his intentions to re-establish the vineyards and become a *vigneron* of high repute.

'We shall become a *mason du vin*!' he firmly stated, smiling contentedly.

'But...' she said, 'I know nothing about wine.'

'Only the taste,' Leo replied ironically.

Marc sat back in his wrought-iron chair. 'Here in Provence, the most popular wine is Châteauneuf-du-Pape. We have the *terroir*, so that classic wine will have competition. We shall have to think hard and come up with an appropriate name. What about Chateau Nuage? What do you think?' he asked.

No one spoke. The revelation came as a complete surprise, leaving Leo dumbstruck.

'Is it your intention for us to be here in the heart of it all?' Karin asked.

'Yes, if you wish. It is your decision,' Marc said, looking at Leo.

'We shall have to sell the flat,' Leo said.

'Why not?' Marc asked. 'It will be a family enterprise, as it was when Papa was alive.' He stood up. 'Let's have dinner.'

Dinner was served late due to their lengthy discussions. Disappointed, Leo had hoped to see the Professor close up at the table. He was sorry she sat at the opposite end, near to Marc. Usually Karin was at her worst when she was at a table with a gathering of guests. Marc was astonished at her change of behaviour. Leo was filled with relief. He had wondered earlier if she would force her presence on to Madelaine, but in this instance she was calm and amiable, enjoying conversation with another guest on her right. He noticed she was drinking mineral water.

Leo was full of the outcome of his meeting with Marc, which had brought pleasing results for both of them. The scheme for reinstating wine production interested him and the project was an exciting one. Marc had suggested that he and Karin should move to France and live on the estate in a cottage, to be made ready for them. There were many prospects that Leo could not ignore and he hoped Karin would be in agreement: a new house, a new family member, a fresh start – the future was full of promise and there would be money in the bank.

Marc had initially regarded his relative's visit as an inconvenience. They had been amazed at the state of Nuage, and despite Marc's efforts to explain and describe the situation, his attempts to dissuade them had failed. Karin and the boys were thrown into the mess, chaos and unknown land where the natives spoke a strange language.

Simone had good news from Crispin who telephoned his parents daily. Karin spent most of her time in the safety of the room Marc had allocated them. To be free to roam around was too hazardous and she feared for their safety.

Madelaine had been busy, occupied with the task she had to complete and loving every minute of it. It was necessary to be preoccupied with the project and she was continually distracted by thoughts of the Comte and the way he had kissed her. Secretly she scolded herself for how she had responded. It was obvious that they were both attracted to one another and the following days were full of proof of their mutual desire.

Marc had no wish to dwell on his past period of celibacy. Madelaine's covert liaison with a German Major resulted in a pleasant, almost innocent, relationship. Her friendship with him was built on the necessities of life in occupied France. He supplied her with food and, quite often, small luxuries. He supervised her work and decided on her salary, providing her with a temporary feeling of security. This gave her a tentative satisfaction that she was desired; there was no one else in her lonely life. He had tried unsuccessfully on her behalf to locate her father, but now she hoped she had found a man who might offer what she had felt with longing, after suffering the years of grief. To her it was obvious that the Comte was lonely and, like so many others, had a shattered mind and suffered from bouts of depression, induced by periods of hate and bitter memories, with thoughts of revenge. She decided she would give him any assistance that he needed. He had a case to answer and she would fight for this man until the bitter end.

The future of Nuage lay partly in their abilities to negotiate a fair and acceptable settlement. Each of them hoped the time they spent together would never end. The days became idyllic, until the hateful day arrived when she had to return to Paris, encumbered with an enormous file on Nuage, and her own private one of the pictures. She had fallen in love with Nuage – Provence, with all its beauty, had left her with magical memories. Saddened that the day of departure was with them, Marc wanted to go with her to Paris, but circumstances were too difficult, and she declined his offer.

'I'll telephone you before dinner,' he said, his voice loud due to an arriving train on the platform. Apart from the files, she had only a small amount of luggage, which he swiftly put on board. Then he put his arm around her and held her close. She kissed his cheek, her perfume filling his nostrils with its seductive scent.

'I love you,' he whispered. 'I'll come to Paris very soon.'

'Or I'll visit London,' she said.

'Yes, please,' he answered, as she pulled away.

The guard blew a whistle and the claxon hooted.

'Marc!' she said urgently. 'Be careful, won't you.'

'I'm always careful,' he answered. 'Especially now I've got a good reason.'

He did not wait for the train to pull away, his life had changed, and he knew the next few days were going to be hell without her.

26

To Marc's concern, Germaine had been behaving out of character for several weeks. He too had become a changed man. Everyone had noticed the alterations in his life, but only one of them suspected the cause. In her desperation to speak to him, Germaine found it almost impossible to get him on his own. There was always someone who sought his attention, usually builders or the two boys. Before the Professor left, she received his attention. Germaine had seen how they looked at each other, never missing their small, intimate moments. He could not stop himself from what he was doing – he had invested his life in a beautiful woman whom he hoped would return his love. Because of her, the hate and anger dissipated into a distant darkness that had occupied his mind, and was replaced by her entering his life.

Leo was satisfied with his visit and the conclusion drawn from long talks with his brother. The decision to re-establish the vineyards and the planned production of wine excited him. At last he had been given the opportunity to assert himself, putting him on a level with his older brother. It would be good to get out of London and to join Marc, becoming an enterprising entrepreneur.

The subject of their adopting a child had become an additional reason. Marc had no children. It was doubtful if he ever would have a child. Should he survive Marc, he would succeed him and become the Comte Chevaud. Thoughts on this subject terrified him. Leo knew he had to return to the UK for an important meeting with the adoption agency. With the situation permanently on his mind, he went to find Marc.

Marc was in the builders' hut with Germaine when Leo joined them, and she was annoyed at the interruption. It was the same old scene – catching Marc on his own was almost impossible. She went to the door to leave.

'No Germaine, please stay, as there are things I need to discuss with you regarding the estate.'

She turned round to face him, seeing the earnest expression on his face. Leo pulled out a chair for her and then seated himself, waiting for the right moment to tell Marc of his decision.

'Marc, we have to go back to England to meet our future child's social worker. We will take Piers and Crispin with us.'

'Of course, I'll arrange the flight for you. Keep in touch, I will look forward to becoming an uncle again.'

Leo took a deep breath and left hurriedly.

'Marc,' Germaine pressed, 'it is starting to get on top of me. I hate to say it, but I can't cope.'

'Oh, I'm sorry. I too have given it much thought.'

'Any ideas?'

'Yes, Philippe has to have a permanent carer, someone with more experience. Marie-Jeanne is too young and emotionally involved. She does a fair job in the crêperie, but not so good with her grandfather.'

Marc suggested to Germaine that Marie-Jeanne accompany Leo and Karin back to England, where she could become an au pair, helping Karin with the adopted child. A nurse would be engaged for Philippe.

'Germaine, we will be able to find a nurse for Philippe. Marie-Jeanne will be able to stand on her own two feet, she will discover the world.'

Germaine was sitting, staring at her clasped hands in her lap. 'A qualified nurse would be expensive. I don't have that sort of money and neither does he. The crêperie is dead during the winter, with little money taken.'

201

He looked at her kindly and smiled. 'You won't have to pay anything, leave that to me.'

'A nurse would have to live in, and there's not enough room in his cottage.'

'That problem can be overcome.'

'You think so?' she asked.

Marc pulled open a drawer, pulled out a pack of cheroots and sat twisting one in his hand. 'I think you have the answer to that question.'

A deep frown of misunderstanding formed between her brows.

He inhaled blue smoke and the aroma of tobacco filled the small prefabricated room. He smiled at her, that lovely open smile which reached his eyes when he was a carefree youth. 'I believe you know exactly what I imply. It is simple, Germaine. You move from your place into Philippe's.' As an afterthought, he added. 'You can become his resident carer. You know how to handle him.'

'He is a stubborn old fool,' she remarked.

'He is no fool. Stubborn yes. I shall need your cottage initially for my brother's family, until we come to a reciprocal arrangement. You will live as you have always done, rent-free and enjoying all the privileges of being employed by the estate. I shall, of course, pay you a good salary. No more crêpes.'

'You mean you no longer need me here at Nuage?'

'Not as much as Philippe needs you. Do you find my proposition acceptable?'

'Yes,' she answered, 'but supposing Marie-Jeanne refuses to go to England?'

Marc burst out laughing. 'Highly doubtful, she will jump at the chance, as any young girl would. She can't get away from here quick enough.' He stood up, his right hand outstretched. She joined him, taking his hand and gripping it tightly.

'Agreed,' she said, still tightening her grip, as a gesture of gratitude.

27

Marc asked Remy to take Karin, Leo and the boys in the van to the airport. Marie-Jeanne watched their departure from the temporary prefabricated office, her feelings confused. Germaine had spoken to her of Marc's plans for her and Philippe. She took a while to understand the explanation Germaine had given her regarding the sudden and unexpected change. She was, she admitted to herself, rather scared, the excitement of going to London had vanished in the face of the daunting plan to care for a child. Her knowledge in that field was negligible; caring for her grandfather was an entirely different proposition, and the whole prospect added to her nervousness while she waited for her passport to arrive.

Germaine suggested that Marie-Jeanne ask Marc to tell her about life in London, and when he did so her spirits rose to a higher plain. His advice was long in delivery and she listened intently as he related points concerning Leo and Karin which were relevant and would help the girl's future. Like her late elder sister, she was of peasant stock but, just as Sylvie had been, she was very pretty and with a gregarious nature. After all, alone in a strange city, with only basic knowledge of the language, while living in a select apartment in a fashionable part of London, anything could happen. Marie-Jeanne was gullible, an innocent in London.

At the end of their discussion, Marc showed her out, poured himself a glass of wine and sat down at his desk. Taking a photograph of Madelaine from a drawer, he stared at it with wistful endearing eyes and a craving for her presence.

Finishing his drink, he propped the photo against another

of Simone and Charles, picked up the telephone and dialled a Paris number. He could not hold back the disappointment he felt when Madelaine's secretary explained that the Professor was in Vienna until the next day. He refrained from leaving a message, just requesting her to contact him when she could.

Sitting tapping his fingers on the desk, he came to a decision. He quickly left the temporary site and headed for the crêperie, as the urge to talk to Germaine was great. The crêperie was half-filled with tourists and one or two locals. She raised a hand in greeting.

'I have to speak to you,' he said.

'What, now?' she asked. 'I'm rather busy.'

'Get Marie-Jeanne, isn't she meant to be working here?'

'Not for much longer,' she complained.

'Please Germaine, this affects us all.' His words were spoken in a pleading manner and made her stop what she was doing. She went to the main door to turn the open sign to 'closed'. A customer was courteously refused more coffee. Taking the hint, he walked out, grumbling to impatient customers, who followed suit.

'Funny these people,' a foreigner remarked making for the door.

'Best to talk in the back,' Germaine said, taking a bottle of burgundy.

'Where is Marie-Jeanne?' he enquired.

'With Philippe. She reads to him and he loves it.'

They sat facing each other with the wine in front of them.

'Well?' she asked.

'I have to go to London very shortly,' he explained.

'Will you be coming back?'

'Of course,' he replied. 'I can't just walk away from Nuage and all the mess. My trip concerns Nuage. I have to arrange to pay many people, including you.'

'I'm sure Marie-Jeanne will send money from England when she is working there.' With those words she burst into tears.

He poured her a glass of wine. 'Here drink this, don't cry. It will all come to a satisfying conclusion, wait and see.' Her tears embarrassed him. Germaine had been in his life for a long time, she had been his housekeeper and his mother's loyal confidante.

'How can you be so sure, can you make miracles?'

'*Oui, si je puis,*' he said.

With the corner of her apron, she wiped her tears. 'There is something else you want to say, isn't there?'

A wistful smile broke on his face. Germaine was regarded as a formidable character but she had a huge heart and a quick-thinking mind.

'Yes,' he said, 'but it is highly confidential.'

'I understand,' she said.

'I hope to be married in London,' he murmured, his words barely audible, 'and my wife will be coming back here with me.' He raised his glass, finishing his wine. 'There will be a new Madame la Comtesse, Germaine!'

'Am I allowed to know who she is?'

'I think you already know,' he said, smiling again.

'Yes,' she said. 'I thought she was charming.'

He nodded in approval, played with his empty glass, pushed it across the table and stood up.

'I must get on,' she said. 'Is Remy taking Marie-Jeanne to the airport?'

'No, Benoit is.'

'I will explain to Philippe when she has left.'

'Would you prefer that I do that?' he asked.

'No,' she answered. 'I'll do it. Maybe Marie-Jeanne already has. The story she is reading is taking much longer than usual and he seems to be settled in his own home.'

For reply, Marc shook his head. 'I'm off to sort out a few things with the tiler.' He paused, reached inside his jacket pocket, and tossed an envelope on to the table.

'That's for you, and something to give Marie-Jeanne.' With

a farewell gesture of his hand, he left her to finish her wine and get back to her counter.

'*Bonne chance*,' she said.

It took him longer than he had hoped to finalise outstanding matters but, pleased with the results, he completed packing a small suitcase and locked his briefcase. Before leaving, he had a brief conference with Remy and a few men gathered outside. As with Germaine, Marc had full confidence in Remy, who would talk things over with Benoit on his return. Benoit was a fast driver and knew Marie-Jeanne had a plane to catch. Glancing at his watch, he thought she would have arrived at the airport by now. Any moment Leo would phone to tell him she had arrived and was OK.

Within minutes his assumption was proved right; they chatted, Marc enquiring how Karin was, while Leo fed more coins into the phone box and described how she was feeling better with medication. He spoke of closing the deposit account at the bank before making a hasty goodbye, keeping a watchful eye on Marie-Jeanne, standing outside the glass booth. Walking away, he carried her bags, guiding her through the pressing crowds still waiting at the arrivals gate.

The next day, Marc took the first available flight to Paris and a cab to Madelaine's office. No matter what happened, he knew he would never forget the surprised expression on her face, as her secretary showed him into the book-lined room. Flowers he had sent her were in several vases, displayed in strategic positions. The secretary discreetly left them, but not before she saw him take Madelaine in his arms.

'Why didn't you tell me?'

'I rang your secretary and left a message for you, but you didn't call me.'

'I'm sorry,' she apologised. 'I've been snowed under. Look

at my desk.' She waved her hand in the direction of a tabletop covered with files.

'I have to go to London – will you come with me?'

'What, now? I don't think that's possible!' she replied.

'Do you have my file finished?' he asked.

'Yes, just about. It's been an enormous task, I had to go to Berlin and Vienna.'

'Why have you been there? I have never been to Vienna. Which do you prefer?'

'I hate Vienna, the ghastly Strauss music and cream cakes do nothing for me. The place was crawling with fascists and men in dark glasses and silly hats, reminiscent of Gestapo. It's still a hot house of Nazism and I never want to go there again.'

'Tell me,' he asked curiously, 'about your discoveries there.'

'The Americans are making a new road in the region, at a place called Aut Aussee where there are immense salt mines. A huge treasure trove of Impressionist and Renaissance works of art was discovered. I had to have help, so an expert from London flew over to assist me.' She paused and shook her head. 'And in my humble opinion, I could not put a value on it. It is not possible!'

'That makes mine look unimportant, however, will you come to London with me?' he asked again.

She hesitated, then said, 'Yes, we can go fully prepared.'

'My sister, Simone, has asked us to stay with her.'

'That would be lovely,' she said, kissing his cheek. 'Far nicer than staying in an impersonal hotel.'

'You'll like Simone,' he said, stroking her hair.

'If she's anything like you, I shall love her.'

He released her with regret and watched her collect documents which lay on the desk.

Turning around, her arms full of files, she said, 'I'm ready!' She gave him one of her smiles, which brought him a sense of ecstasy and joy.

Simone was thrilled with the news that Leo gave her. Not only did she have her sons coming home, but her wonderful big brother was returning from France. Leo suggested she could fetch the boys the next morning, when she dropped Charles at his office.

Later that evening her animated behaviour was out of character. Charles was pleasantly relieved to find her more relaxed than usual. She had not been her normal self, separated from her sons for so long, who were now staying overnight with Leo and Karin in Marc's flat, as Leo's was up for sale and the furniture in a repository. During the day, Leo had taken the boys to the Planetarium, solar interest brought on by a telescope Charles had bought during their absence. His own latest hobby of star-searching was far less energetic than a round of golf.

Alone with Karin, Simone sat by the window, in the bedroom which had formerly been Marc's, and made general talk with her about her trip to Mirabeau and how the rebuilding was progressing. She showed a lot of interest, as her own childhood memories of the place were faint.

Marc, tight-lipped as usual, was not generous with information, and Simone was starved of news.

'I'm surprised you don't know of these things, but Marc is the silent type.'

'Yes, I suppose he had to be during the war, as his work demanded it.'

'I don't understand, what did he do?' Karin asked.

'He was in the Free French Army under de Gaulle. Charles believed it was a false cover for something else.'

'Perhaps Leo knew,' Karin said.

Simone gave a short contemptuous laugh. 'Marc would be the last person to speak of his war exploits – my eldest brother is the soul of discretion. Now,' she bent down to feel a radiator. 'Are you warm enough? I think it's ice cold in here. I want to hear about Nuage and what is happening.'

'Something definitely is!' Karin admitted. 'Why do you think Marc is suddenly coming to London?'

'I've no idea.' Simone said. 'He'll probably tell me in good time. Who knows, where Marc is concerned.'

'Leo knows more than he cares to admit, ask him.' She sat on the bed. 'Piers and Crispin will know more. Children are quick to sense atmosphere and unusual happenings.'

Simone smiled to herself. Karin had changed a lot.

'As you will find out, they have a canny way of discovering secrets.'

Karin asked if Simone knew of the Professor he was bringing with him. 'Oh yes, you're in for a surprise, Simone.'

'That's not good enough! Marc was noncommittal when I asked him. I need to know now, to do things the proper way.'

'You always do,' Karin said, slightly grudgingly. 'She is very clever.'

Simone was very surprised that Madelaine was not of the masculine sex.

'Wait and see,' Karin said. 'We all liked her very much, Marc in particular.'

Simone had to accept Karin's words, a little annoyed that she was no better informed. The doorbell rang and her two sons dashed in, their arms full of packages.

'They spent all their pocket money,' Leo said, 'And I had to give them an advance.'

'I'll take them home now, Leo,' Simone said, helping Piers with parcels. 'Crisp, put these in the car, here's the key.' She followed Leo into the kitchen as he started to make some tea. 'What time are they arriving?' She asked.

'Sometime this evening. Marc telephoned from the airport.'

'Leo, I must go, I've left Mary, my daily, with an enormous list. I assumed that the Professor was male, so we shall have to change the sleeping arrangements. Do you think it will be in order for Marc to share a bed with a Professor?'

209

'I'm sure they wouldn't want it any other way,' Karin replied.

'I think Karin's concerned that the interview goes well tomorrow, Leo. I hope I haven't worn her out.'

'It's all right,' he said, pouring tea. 'She's tougher than she looks.'

28

Tactfully, Simone invited Madelaine to see their Hampshire garden. Compared with those of Nuage it was typically suburban. She felt it was an acceptable excuse for the two of them to be alone without interruptions. As Marc knew she would, she found Madelaine fascinating; the woman's knowledge was amazing. Her conversation flowed easily and Simone listened with interest. In turn, she related a potted history of Marc, omitting many wartime anecdotes. Natural curiosity overtook her: if her brother had found someone to share his remaining life, she needed an answer.

'Do you intend to return to Nuage with my brother?'

'Yes,' Madelaine said. 'There is a great deal of work there for me. But first, we have to prepare for the auction.'

'Will that be held in London?' Simone asked. 'I should like to attend.'

'No, I believe we shall have to go to New York.'

'Oh,' Simone replied, slightly baffled. 'I was wondering what your own plans were.'

'My plans are involved with Marc's. Our most important one is that we would like to marry.'

'Oh,' Simone repeated. 'I see.' The last comment was with some surprise, as she hadn't picked up from her previous conversation with Karin that this was such a serious relationship for them both.

'I hope it all goes well, and I wish you success in your venture,' Simone said, pulling her cardigan round her shoulders. Shivering slightly, she took Madelaine's arm and continued, 'It is chilly out here, shall we go back?'

211

Simone had not learned much from talking to Madelaine.

From where they were, Marc could be seen, talking with Charles in the conservatory. Both men waved a hand in greeting. The two men had gleaned more in talking as Marc felt he knew Charles well enough to seek his confidence. He doubted Simone's acceptance of his plans, but waited for her and Madelaine's opinion and their acceptance of each other.

True, both women had much in common; it was his wish that they would become close friends. As they approached, Marc asked his final question.

'Charles, would you consider being best man at our wedding?'

Charles's face remained impassive and he held out a hand to shake Marc's. 'I'd prefer to give the bride away! I assume that will be Leo,' he said resignedly, and walked off to find a bottle of champagne in the pantry, where it was always reliably cold.

They all spent the following day and part of the night discussing plans for the marriage, and developments at Nuage. The estate in general and finances concerning it were huge. The art treasures were only lightly mentioned. No mention of the German occupation or wartime events was made at any time.

Charles had agreed that Piers and Crispin should not be present. Fortunately there was a school sports event that Sunday in which Piers was participating. Eager to be absent, Crispin jumped at the suggestion that he should escort his young brother, a promising athlete, to the meeting. Simone sent them off with a large picnic hamper to get them through the day. It would be far more acceptable to them than a boring session amongst adults discussing adult subjects.

The gathering was to discuss the wedding, and Marc knew that Simone would be the one who would oversee such an occasion. He looked across the table, seeing that she was in her element. Madelaine sat carefully listening to her, and her opinion of church weddings, as opposed to register office, was politely considered.

'The village church! There is a dear little church, here in the village.'

'Simone,' Marc said, 'it is Anglican. Perhaps Madelaine would prefer a Catholic ceremony? I will personally arrange that and find a venue in London.'

Madelaine gave him a glance of gratitude for his diplomacy. Saying nothing, Marc nodded in agreement, looking at Madelaine as she smiled at him. All this chat was immaterial as she and Marc had already discussed plans for their special day, but did not wish to hurt anyone else's feelings.

Before they bade each other goodnight, Charles opened several bottles of champagne. Simone, seated at the dining-room table, casually poured herbal tea. Everyone was relaxed, which pleased her. Madelaine was in deep conversation with Charles.

The ceremony took place in London at the French embassy. Marc had arranged for a priest to officiate, with witnesses being Charles and a Secretary from the Embassy, who by happy coincidence happened to be Madelaine's distant cousin. Their honeymoon continued in London, visiting the offices and salerooms of Sotheby's and Christie's, and a few reputable galleries, while staying at the Savoy Hotel. Simone was disappointed that they had declined her offer to stay with her, so she suggested that she drive them to Heathrow, for their return flight to Paris.

During the weeks they had been in London, work at Nuage had been non-stop. Labourers and craftsmen worked round the clock, spurred on by the promise of extra pay as bonuses. The progress on the house was incredible.

It was dusk when Marc and Madelaine reached Nuage. As the taxi turned round, the tyres crunching on newly-laid gravel, a sudden unexpected sequence of lights illuminated the façade, bathing the chateau in a scene of brilliance.

Madelaine gasped, taking Marc's arm. They were both speechless with surprise.

'*Son et lumière*!' she cried.

Figures came running from the main door, waving and shouting. Without warning, several lights went out. A single floodlight was switched on, lighting the main entrance and portico. It forced its powerful beam on two figures waiting to climb down the six wide steps. With precise caution, Germaine slowly made her way down, one arm round the other person's waist, steering his hesitant body. Marc waited for them to reach level ground before he stepped forward. He could hardly believe what he was seeing, the bright light dazzled his eyes, but he knew who it was, clinging to Germaine and holding a walking stick.

Marc's sight was not improved by the tears he felt trickling down his face. Madelaine heard him sob.

'Darling,' she said, 'go to him, he's waiting for you.'

'Come with me,' his choked reply came back.

The gathered crowd of onlookers stood in silence. When they reached Germaine's side, she said, 'Gently Marc, he's still very fragile.'

'Of course.' He moved in front of Philippe, taking his stick from him. 'You don't need this, old friend. My arm is just as reliable.'

Apart from movement made by their hands, wiping the tears from their eyes, Madelaine and Germaine stood motionless in the floodlights, to listen to two adult men in the autumn of their years as they struggled to find suitable words.

'I must get him back to his bed,' Germaine said. 'All this excitement could be bad for him.'

'Let us take him,' Madelaine suggested.

Unsure, Germaine hesitated. 'Yes, he would like that.'

Philippe grunted his answer. More lights were switched on, joined by a well-worn recording of 'La Marseillaise'. Madelaine, now openly weeping, stood with a handkerchief to her face.

It was all too much for many of the spectators. Some had slowly started to walk away. Remy dropped to his knees, the emotion of the moment causing him to suddenly think of his brother's decapitated head lying in a pool of blood. Pushing away these memories was hard, as he had been very close to his brother, and they flooded his mind.

Marc steered Philippe's unsteady body to the waiting horse and cart Benoit had left by the side gates. The open tailboard enabled Marc and others to lift Philippe into the cart.

Madelaine helped put Philippe to bed. Her capabilities and caring nature did not go unnoticed by Marc. Later she found Marc at the bottom of Philippe's cottage garden, smoking a cigar and staring at the starlit sky. Hearing her footsteps, he turned with his arms outstretched, the cigar dropping to the ground.

'I'm sorry, I didn't mean to abandon you, I'm sorry,' he said.

'There's nothing to forgive. May I just say, *thank you.*'

'No, I must thank *you.*'

'Goodness me, for what?' she asked.

'For coming into my life and bringing back happiness.' He drew her close and kissed her. 'I love you,' he whispered.

'It is such a beautiful night – can we walk for a while?'

'Yes, that's a wonderful idea,' he replied. 'We'll go to the main gates and check them. Is that too far for you?'

'No,' she said, laughing. 'I could walk all night. I am so very, very happy.'

When they reached the high, imposing gates, their pace slowed until they stopped to peer through the decorative wrought-iron patterns. The gates had miraculously survived, unlike everything else metallic, which had been stolen for the German war machine.

'What's out there?' she asked, her voice fading into the darkness.

'Our world,' he replied.

'I want to thank you for everything.'

He placed an arm around her waist and became silent, his thoughts slipping back across the years that had passed, lingering on the most recent events.

'Welcome home, Marc,' she said.

'Thank you,' he replied. 'You have given me all I shall ever need. Because of you, I'm here. If only you knew how often I'd prayed for this moment. During the dark days, thoughts like this kept me sane and possibly alive. I used to fantasise a lot.'

'No more talk of the dark days,' she said. 'We are strong enough to chase away the shadows.'

He pulled her closer. 'I love you.' He bent his head to kiss her hair.

Some shadows never go away, they persistently hover, as did the hateful memories. There would be constant reminders. Philippe was still in his life – Nuage and Mirabeau – some of the images of evil would never begin to fade. The killings, torture and deceit by those who had been considered to be good friends, but had betrayed him and others to the enemy – they all belonged to the shadows of yesterday. If he could change time, he would. Looking ahead, he would concentrate on tomorrow, which he would share with Madelaine. He was no longer alone, living with yesterday, together they would share tomorrow.

His laughter sounded across the reclaimed gardens, competing with the repaired fountain, gurgling with trickling water. The carved marble boy blew his silent horn to an audience of contented carp, cautiously navigating their recently acquired new home – a vast improvement on their overcrowded glass tank in a pet shop in Arles. They replaced their predecessors who had been unfortunate enough to become a rare delicacy for starving German soldiers.

Marc suddenly burst into fresh laughter. The scene of the fountain and the carved figure reminded him of a painting by Monet.

'Can you explain the joke?' Madelaine asked.

'All these pictures the Germans stole. The joke is that they were all fakes. You have seen the genuine ones. My late father was a very clever man.'

'I must study the inventories of the main auction houses. The fakes may not come up for sale. Shall we go to some sales, when I've searched the catalogues?'

He stopped laughing. 'Of course, but we shan't bid for any.'

'Certainly,' she replied and smiled into the darkness. 'There is no need when we have the real thing!'

'Home!' he said in the moonlight. 'Welcome home, Madame la Comtesse. I should carry you over the threshold. May I?'

Nervously, she giggled from excitement. 'Don't drop me!'

'Never!' His final words floated away on the still magical air. The old clock, a relic of Napoleonic history, chimed the hour of midnight, announcing the arrival of another day. Yesterday had gone.

Glossary

à demain	Tomorrow.
bar des pêcheurs	Fisherman's bar.
bar tabac	Bar selling tobacco.
bien sur	Of course.
Boche	A derogatory term for German soldiers.
bonne chance	Good luck.
boules	A game using metal balls which are aimed at a target.
Cappello hat	A hat with a wide, circular brim and a rounded crown, worn outdoors in some countries by Catholic clergy, when dressed in a cassock.
caves	Cellars.
cerf	A type of deer.
chassé	Ballet dance, gliding triple-step pattern.
cheroot	A cheap cylindrical cigar with both ends clipped during manufacture.
Comtesse	Countess.
Cours Lavantre	A square in Arles.
crêperie	Pancake café.
déjà vu	Already seen before.
domage	Pity.
Führer	Leader.
Gauleiter	The party leader of a regional branch of the NSDAP (more commonly known as the Nazi Party).

Gestapo	Official secret police of Nazi Germany.
grand mal du malfaisant	Evil.
Grandpère	Grandfather.
J'espére que tu vas bien	I hope you are well.
La Marseillaise	French national anthem.
Laissez-moi, s'il vous plait!	Leave me alone!
Le Monde	'The World': a French newspaper.
Louis Quinze chairs	Louis XV (1723–1774), highly ornamental, yet elegant furniture.
Madame la Comtesse	Madam, the Countess.
Maquis/Maquisard	French resistance fighters.
Marc	A grape pomace brandy which is a highly intoxicating spirit, illegally distilled.
merci	Thank you.
Milice	Militia.
Monsieur le Comte	The Count.
Mon Seigneur	My Lord.
Musée des Peintures	Museum of Paintings.
pas de deux	Ballet dance for two people symbolising partnership.
Père	Father.
Pernod	Aniseed flavour liqueur.
privé	Private, undisturbed.
Proveneux	A native from Provence.
Reeperbahn	Red light district in Hamburg.
salauds	Bastards.
sangliers	Wild boar.
sens unique	One-way street.
son et lumière	A sound and light show, usually outdoors at night.
tablier	Apron.

terroir	Earth.
toilette turque	A primitive ancient lavatory consisting of a hole with iron foot plates on each side.
une table profonde	A secluded table.
venez-moi	Come!
verderers	Officials in Britain who deal with common land in certain former royal hunting areas which are the property of the Crown.
vigneron	Cultivator of grapes for wine.
voila!	There it is!
Waffen-SS	The armed wing of the Nazi Party's Schutzstaffel ('Protective Squadron').
Wehrmacht	The armed services of the Third Reich.
Zinc	An area of a bar made of marble and zinc. The expression was used in large Paris bars where customers waited to be served, disregarding waiter service and hence avoiding having to pay extra and/or a tip.
Zut!	Dash it!/Botheration!